And I was so glad I did.

He said he would make me happy. And I was so glad he said that to me.

He shared all this happiness with me. That's why I'm certain—

No matter what anyone says, I am the happiest girl in the world.

WORLDEND

WHAT DO YOU DO AT THE END OF THE WORLD?

ARE YOU BUSY? WILL YOU SAVE US?

3 **Akira Kareno**
Illustrations by ue

Nopht
Keh
Desperatio

"Then tell me,
how valiant
was Chtholly?"

When I was born, huh...?
I can't say much about it. No, I'm not being mean; I just don't remember.
I feel like I was asleep for several months after I was born.

So, right. I know what my oldest memory is.
It's of Rhan's face, peering at mine with a big ol' grin.
"*You're awake! She's awake!*" she said.
She was super-happy.
When I saw her, I somehow felt better, too. I started cackling and
couldn't stop.
Well, yep. I guess that'd be my oldest memory.
...What? Why are you grinning like that? Did I say something funny?

I was excited.
A feeling of wonder, of what might happen next, of what cheer might be waiting in this world, spread throughout my heart.

Huh? Why are you looking at me like that?
We were talking about how I felt right after I was born, right?
I was just answering your question.

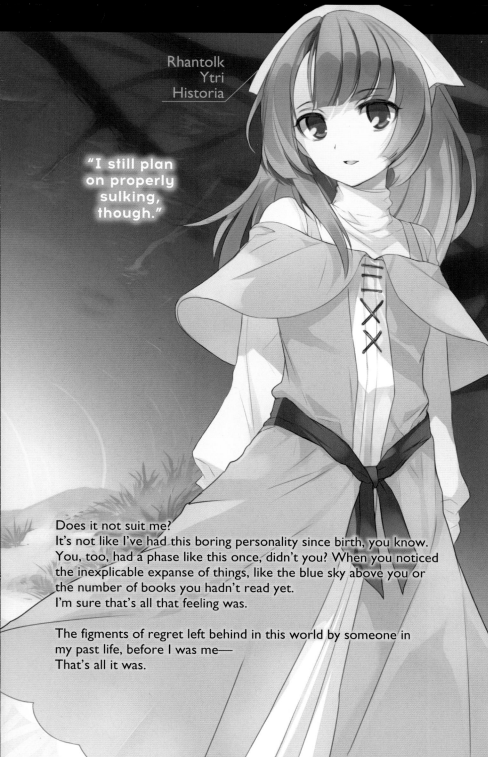

Rhantolk
Ytri
Historia

"I still plan
on properly
sulking,
though."

Does it not suit me?
It's not like I've had this boring personality since birth, you know.
You, too, had a phase like this once, didn't you? When you noticed
the inexplicable expanse of things, like the blue sky above you or
the number of books you hadn't read yet.
I'm sure that's all that feeling was.

The figments of regret left behind in this world by someone in
my past life, before I was me—
That's all it was.

The future is always in our hands.

What slips between our fingers is what we call the past.

Willem

Glick

One person's great ambitions are another person's reality. That's how the two of us are connected.

WORLDEND

WHAT DO YOU DO AT THE END OF THE WORLD?

ARE YOU BUSY? WILL YOU SAVE US?

#03

AKIRA KARENO

Illustrations by **ue**

YEN
ON

NEW YORK

WORLDEND: WHAT DO YOU DO AT THE END OF THE WORLD? ARE YOU BUSY? WILL YOU SAVE US?

AKIRA KARENO

Translation by Jasmine Bernhardt
Cover art by ue

SHUMATSU NANI SHITEMASUKA? ISOGASHIIDESUKA? SUKUTTEMORATTEIIDESUKA? Vol. 3
©2015 Akira Kareno, ue
First published in Japan in 2015 by KADOKAWA CORPORATION, Tokyo.
English translation rights arranged with KADOKAWA CORPORATION, Tokyo, through TUTTLE-MORI AGENCY, INC., Tokyo.

English translation © 2019 by Yen Press, LLC

Yen On
1290 Avenue of the Americas
New York, NY 10104

Visit us at yenpress.com ▪ facebook.com/yenpress ▪ twitter.com/yenpress ▪
yenpress.tumblr.com ▪ instagram.com/yenpress

First Yen On Edition: March 2019

Yen On is an imprint of Yen Press, LLC.
The Yen On name and logo are trademarks of Yen Press, LLC.

Library of Congress Cataloging-in-Publication Data
Names: Kareno, Akira, author. I ue, illustrator. I Bernhardt, Jasmine, translator.
Title: WorldEnd : what do you do at the end of the world? are you busy? will you save us? / Akira Kareno ;
   illustration by ue ; translation by Jasmine Bernhardt.
Other titles: WorldEnd. English
Description: First Yen On edition. I New York : Yen On, 2018– I Subtitle translated from Shumatsu Nani
   Shitemasuka? Isogashiidesuka? Sukuttemoratteiidesuka?
Identifiers: LCCN 2018016690 I ISBN 9781975326876 (v. 1 : pbk.) I ISBN 9781975326883 (v. 2 : pbk.) I
   ISBN 9781975326913 (v. 3 : pbk.)
Classification: LCC PZ7.1.K364 Wo 2018 I DDC [Fic]—dc23
LC record available at https://lccn.loc.gov/2018016690

ISBNs: 978-1-9753-2691-3 (paperback)
       978-1-9753-2692-0 (ebook)

10 9 8 7 6 5 4 3 2 1

LSC-C

Printed in the United States of America

WorldEnd

WHAT DO YOU DO AT THE END OF THE WORLD?

ARE YOU BUSY? WILL YOU SAVE US?

WORLDEND

WHAT DO YOU
DO AT THE END
OF THE WORLD?

ARE YOU BUSY?
WILL YOU SAVE US?

#03
contents

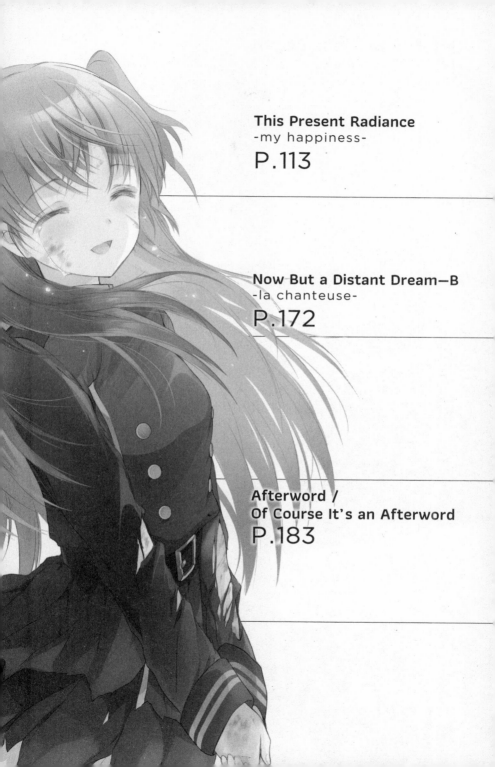

Before That War Began
-legal braves-

It was the eve of the final battle.

Everyone decided they should at least spend their last night with the people they missed the most.

The legendary band of heroes who had gathered to subdue the Visitor Elq Hrqstn, designated enemy of the Church of Exalted Light, temporarily disbanded for that very reason.

"...So why did you come to see me anyway?"

Her former master, whom she hadn't seen in a long while, asked the question with a frown.

"'Cause I don't have any lovers or family, y'know?"

Lillia cackled as she answered.

They were in a shantytown in the corner of the Imperial Capital's sixth district, far removed from the knights' regular patrol routes. The inn where her master chose to stay was located on a block notorious for rampant pickpocketing.

The floor creaked loudly with every step. Dust caked the hearths to the point that they were unusable. All of the installed lamps were almost out of oil, and none of them offered very good light. Five silver coins for a night at a place like this sounded like highway robbery, but there was value in the goat-head design carved on the bottom half of the sign that hung out front. Put simply, the area's influential organization, known as the Whisperers, guaranteed peace and quiet to any who stayed here.

"I was trying to think of someone who's like family to me, but the only person I could come up with was you, master! Geez, what a lonely life I've lived, right?"

Lillia burst into forced laughter.

Her master was a man of many mysteries. He had a slim build, but it was hard to tell his age... He could pass for thirty or sixty years old either way. Lillia had first met him over ten years ago, and his appearance hadn't changed very much. It almost looked like he was getting younger.

His age wasn't the only unknown; his birth and upbringing were also a mystery. He was a master of each and every martial art, though it was anyone's guess as to where he learned them. Moreover, his deep and extensive knowledge was so great that all the scholars in the capital were no match for him.

This man, her master, dropped his shoulders in an exaggerated manner, tired.

"...And what about my senior pupil who you're so fond of?"

"Willem? He said he was going back to Gomag to see Allie and the others."

"You should've gone with him, then. He'd never refuse his adorable junior."

"Ah-ha-ha-ha, you always make the worst jokes, master!" Though she laughed, the crevasses between her brows suddenly deepened. "If I really did ask that idiot, not only would he actually say yes, he might treat me like real family." She lowered her voice as though she wanted to intimidate him.

"Of course he would. What's wrong with that?"

"The world might end."

Silence.

"There's a place that I'd give up anything to go home to, but I know I'll never be able to go back. That's true for me. That's true for you. And it was the same for all the people who came before us. I don't know why, but it's one of the basic conditions for being a Legal Brave, isn't it? It'd be bad news if I had a home to go back to, right?"

"It's not like it's an exact rule, though."

"Still. I can only keep the title of Legal Brave because the Church of

Exalted Light recognized me as the unhappiest person in the world, right? At any rate, that's why I think the second I become the happiest person in the world, I'll be stripped of my qualifications.

"Of course, I think I'd still be able to fight well enough with all this talent and skill at my disposal. But not against the Visitors—not the way a certain *someone* can, that's for sure."

"Wait, you don't think you could be the happiest person in the world *that* easily, do you?"

"I'm confident I could. I'm just lonely, after all."

Silence.

"You said it to me before, didn't you, master? No one can match a Legal Brave's strength. That's why the Legal Brave needs to stay isolated—right? That was all wrong.

"I'm so strong right now that it even scares me. But someone has been constantly following behind me, always. Even though he should know that he'll never catch up, he never gets it. I glance back, and he's always there. It's like a B-class horror story! He's always, always following me. The fool won't leave me alone."

"You hate him that much?" the master asked, annoyed.

"Hmm." Lillia stared into space and searched from within her for what she wanted to say about Willem. "Yeah, I hate how serious he is. He's still a kid on the inside even though his body's grown up; plus, he uses brute force and physical strength in anything he does despite how much he studies; and just because he happened to meet you a bit earlier, he struts around like a senior pupil; and besides, he used to be cute a long time ago, but now he's gotten so tall; then there's the fact that he's not inconsiderate, but he understands nothing about women."

"That's harsh."

That was true. She didn't disagree. She was practically forcing herself to come up with more false accusations as she rambled on.

But what could she do? If she didn't keep it up, then Lillia Asplay would stop hating him. The moment she stopped, there probably wasn't anything she could do to keep herself from falling for him.

Willem Kmetsch was the type of guy who couldn't bear it if the people around him were unhappy. It didn't matter if they were young or old, male or female. If someone said, *"I'm lonely; can you stay with me?"* he would undoubtedly do it. Even if that someone happened to be Lillia Asplay—though he might scrunch up his face in a frown if it was her.

But that would be enough to satisfy her. She would discard the title of the unhappiest person in the world. Then, after that—

"......"

The Church of Exalted Light would mobilize and begin searching for the next suitable person to be the Legal Brave.

She didn't want to think about what would happen after that.

"—Whatever. Whether I'm a backup choice or not, I'm not gonna turn away a pupil who's coming to me on their last night."

As he mussed his own hair, the master grasped his coat from a worn-out chair.

"This ain't the place for a long conversation, so let's continue at a place with food and drink. It'd be the first time in a while I'll be hearing about your least favorite senior pupil's tales of valor."

"Okay, sure. Are there any good places around here?"

"Don't get your hopes up. Most don't serve proper meals." Her master stepped across the creaking floor and placed his hand on the warped door. "That reminds me, Lillia. I'm surprised you found me here. I don't think I've been telling the Alliance what I've been up to recently."

"Hmm? Oh yeah. Finding you was a serious pain."

…That was right. She hadn't been able to track down the master himself at all through conventional methods.

He had been a prestigious knight of the old Dione Order as well as the Eighteenth Legal Brave, once upon a time. She had assumed incorrectly that it would be easy to gather information on sightings of him out in public, given how famous he was.

That was why it was entirely coincidence that she had run into the master here.

She had actually been searching for someone else—the remnants of an armed anti-Empire cult she and the others had decisively taken down the other day, along with a dangerous individual who was developing some kind of new project.

This inn was just one of the places that came up during the course of her investigation.

And staying in this inn, for some reason, was her master, who she hadn't been able to find no matter how much she'd searched.

She wanted to think it was a coincidence. She wanted to unconditionally trust someone so important to her. But Lillia wasn't so innocent as to drop all suspicions in a situation like this, nor did she lack any responsibility herself.

"Oh yeah, I just remembered I had something else I wanted to ask you."

"Yeah? What?"

She inhaled.

Exhaled.

She calmed her pounding heart and asked:

"Are you the current leader of True World, master?"

Slowly, her master turned around.

He did not respond with words. He didn't need to. Just by the tinge of caution in her master's eyes, Lillia knew her prediction was correct.

But not a single part of her felt happy about it.

Even When the Sun Sets
-slight light, slight hope-

1. Even Further Beneath the Starry Sky

A long time ago, life thrived on the surface.

The trees grew thick, animals ran about, and many people, including the emnetwiht, carried on with their lives.

What so easily destroyed that era of prosperity was what the world afterward called the "Seventeen Beasts." They appeared seemingly from nowhere, completely obliterating anything and everything on land that could be considered "life."

Everyone and everything that once inhabited the surface disappeared.

The emnetwiht, the dragons, the morians, the elves—they were all wiped out. The scant few who managed to escape into the sky narrowly avoided death.

Over five hundred years had passed since then.

The last pocket garden of Regule Aire, where the survivors remained, had still not sunk. They were managing to just barely hold out against repeated attacks by the Beasts.

They borrowed the power of the wishing crystals left behind by the emnetwiht—the Carillon.

And they sent out girls who possessed incredibly fleeting lives to die, one after another.

✝

The low, constant reverberation of the enchanted furnace vibrated deep in her stomach.

Nopht got off the windowsill, thinking how bad it must be for her health.

The world beyond the window was blotted out in total darkness. It now acted like a mirror, and all she could see reflected there was a single child scowling at her, lips in a pout. She had no fun glaring back.

"Ugh! Man, I'm sooo bored! Bored, bored, bored!"

She flopped backward onto the simple cot and kicked her legs about. She knew throwing a tantrum would get her nowhere, but her body still moved of its own accord.

This airship—the surface observation ship *Saxifraga*—now hovered roughly fifty marmer above the ground.

The Seventeen Beasts, the menaces of the surface, could not fly freely. It was estimated they would not be attacked if they kept this altitude.

However, being safe and sound often led to boredom.

"Wasn't the surface supposed to be full of romance and adventure?! What about the falcon princess trapped on an emnetwiht altar, surrounded by a hundred Beasts, waiting for a prince to save her?! What about the mountain of treasure slumbering just beneath the gray sand and the ghosts of bandit kings waiting to possess you?! Why's there nothing but sand and rocks here?! Where's the treasure?! Where're the ghosts?! Where are the Beasts?!"

"Nopht, please shut up."

A quiet voice reprimanded her.

Nopht turned her head to look, and there sitting on the cot beside her was Rhantolk, reading some kind of book.

"What's that?"

"An artifact that emerged from the sand yesterday. I thought it might relieve my boredom, so I *borrowed* it from the cargo hold."

Rhantolk always sounded miserable, and she often spoke in a manner that put distance between her and others. That was why the youngest girls at the warehouse were typically afraid of her or didn't like her... But Nopht thought the girl wasn't so bad once she got to know her.

She didn't think Rhantolk was a *good* person, but then again, the feeling was mutual.

"An ancient manuscript, huh. Can you read it?"

Nopht wrapped her arms around Rhantolk from behind and peered over her shoulder.

It was definitely a book. Though its coloring was a bit off, its binding was sturdy, and it didn't look brittle at all. Maybe it was better preserved than they thought.

She also directed her gaze to what was on the page, but—well, sure enough, it just looked like row after row of unfamiliar symbols.

"Mm… There are some words I understand." Rhantolk plucked out a simple biscuit with her slim fingers. "It's not enough to accurately understand the content. But by stringing together words and imagining what they mean, it's the perfect sort of puzzle to alleviate my boredom."

A slight frown appeared on Rhantolk's face when she felt Nopht's weight hanging on her back.

"Huh. So what's it mean?"

"I'm just telling you what I think it means, okay?"

"Sure, tell me what you think it means. Coming into contact with ancient records and setting my imagination aloft is exciting enough."

Rhantolk sighed, a slight expression of annoyance on her face.

Nopht knew it well. Rhantolk made this face as she complained yet patiently went along with Nopht's selfish requests.

"—The emnetwiht race should never have been started. This was the first and greatest sin of the Visitors, who created them."

"What's that mean?"

"I told you—that's what I imagine this book is talking about. After staring at the introduction for so long, that seems to be what the first line is talking about."

"Huh. If that came from emnetwiht ruins, I guess that means they knew they were bad news, too."

"No, it seems like this was treated as a dangerous idea to the emnetwiht at the time. Perhaps like the heavenward ideology in Regule Aire now."

"Oh."

The heavenward ideology. Nopht had heard of that before.

Basically, the ideology stated that the Regule Aire they lived on now was nothing but a point of passage and that they would have to drift farther away from the corrupted surface and go to the distant stars.

Just saying it brought very little actual harm, but there were more than a few among those who believed it who dirtied their hands trying to steal airships or build airships illicitly, so most islands treated it with caution.

"Then"—Rhantolk's slim finger followed the line on the page—"the beasts...sealed...the people... Oh, I think it's the other way around. The people freed the beasts, and a world filled... No, the world filled with a gray truth...?"

"Ohhh."

Nopht leaned even farther over her shoulder. Consequently, even more of her weight pressed down on Rhantolk's back.

"Nopht, you're heavy."

"So that's when the land was wrecked by the Beasts. Wow, it's like a prophecy."

"You think so? It seems like this was just one of a great many produced, and I think it might have been something like a children's story or a textbook or a doctrine."

"I see."

As she found herself satisfied, Nopht reached forward and "borrowed" one of the biscuits Rhantolk held in her hand. It was dry and crumbly and not very good, but it was perfect for tricking her empty stomach into thinking it was delicious.

"There's still more to this sentence. Um... The sixteen shards...sing the song of...the reimagining of the true world...and salvation for the end...sea and mother...fear...spoiled...a perfected heart...um, the void... dawn...?"

Nopht tilted her head in confusion.

That wasn't a sentence. That was a string of completely unrelated words.

"Where's your imagination?"

"No, it truly is just a line of words here. There's no room for interpretation in the first place, much less imagination—"

There was a knock at the door.

Nopht furrowed her brow and let go of Rhantolk.

The two of them held special status. Everyone on the airship knew that. No one tried to get close to them or interact with them. Consequently, there shouldn't have been anyone aboard who would visit this room. The only exception would be if this airship had encountered unimaginable danger that only the two of them could deal with.

But the ship was much too silent for that. They strained their ears, and the only thing they could hear was the humming of the furnace. They could not hear a single scream or howl or siren or artillery bombardment.

"You can come in; it's unlocked."

Cautious, they called out to whoever was on the other side of the door. The knob turned.

"—Is this the convoy guard waiting room?"

A boggard man slowly peeked into the room.

He wore sturdy clothes, made solely with practicality in mind. He didn't look like he belonged to the military at all. He didn't even seem like a merchant.

"I need to speak to the guard who made preparations for the Beasts' attacks… Hmm? Are you ladies the only ones in here?"

"I don't know who you are, but please leave," Rhantolk replied coolly. "According to fleet regulations, contact between us and the members of the research team is forbidden. The very act of approaching this room should not even be allowed. What is our guard doing?"

"Oh, him? He racked up a lot of debts to me in cards a while ago. I only had to ask, and he looked the other way for me."

The boggard gave a friendly grin and, without a moment's hesitation, stepped into the room.

"Whoops, forgot to introduce myself. I'm Glick. I'm usually a civilian salvager, but today, I've been hired by Orlandry to act as something like an adviser for the research team. Well, I'm not usually in a position like this, but I guess stuff happens… And? What might your names be?"

"You think we'll tell you? We never asked anyway." Nopht rested her cheek on her knees and waved him away.

"You shouldn't defy the Alliance's intentions, especially if you've been hired by them." Rhantolk in turn also waved him off.

"Meh, they're different. Wouldn't you want to say hello to someone who's gonna be watching your back from now on?"

"…You're an odd one, old man." Nopht narrowed her eyes. "The only ones here are us two. As you can see, we're featureless, we're girls, and we're children. Do you think we look like amazing warriors meant to protect the fleet from the terrifying Beasts?"

"To be honest, I kinda both do and don't believe it, but at the same time, I don't want to. But you know"—the boggard pointed to the large sword wrapped in cloth, leaning against the wall—"young ladies with dug weapons sounds too much like a story I've already heard. Leprechauns, was it?"

"Why do you know that?"

"I had the opportunity to hear about them just the other day… And I'm not that old, by the way."

"You're older than us, at least."

Glick's expression indicated he only somewhat agreed with them.

"Oh, right, I brought you guys a present. You probably haven't had anything decent to eat, since you've been on the surface for so long. Here, it's a meat pie I got at a stall at the port right before leaving Island No. 31."

He produced a package and placed it on the table.

Nopht's shoulders shivered, her gaze bore a hole into the package, her mouth watered, and her stomach growled painfully. The boggard was right. It had been more than a month since they left Regule Aire to provide security for the research team, and the only things they'd been eating were dried meats and biscuits—food that was light and easily preserved, offering little in the way of actual taste. She missed real food so, so much.

"It's just common sense for us salvagers to be particular about food if we're gonna be on the surface for a long time. The guy who planned this research stuff is clueless about all this.

"...Oh yeah, I asked them to put more spices in so it'll keep for longer, but you should eat it as soon as possible. Today, if you can."

Nopht gulped.

But she couldn't give in to her appetite right now. She concentrated all her willpower to tear her gaze away from the package. Then, with watering eyes, she glared hard at the boggard.

"You're kidding. There's no way you could win us over with such—"

"Thank you for such a kind gift."

"—obvious bribery... Oh, come *oooooon, Rhaaaaan!*"

The tears spilled from her eyes as she turned to look at her best friend sitting beside her.

"Why are you doing this?! We're not supposed to take it!"

"But it smells delicious. We've been eating biscuits for such a long time—I can't resist the temptation."

"I totally understand how you feel, and my whole body and soul agree with you, but you *caaaaan't!*"

"It's the boggards who have such a different sense of taste than we do, so if we refuse and give it back, the meat pie will just end up going bad. But more importantly..." Rhantolk's gaze sharpened, and she smiled. "We have some free time right now. I don't suppose it would be a terrible idea to have a little chat?"

...*Oh boy, here we go.*

Nopht knew that nothing else she could say would matter.

Once Rhantolk started playing the role of devil's advocate, there was no one in the world who could change her mind. About six months ago, even when she and that stubborn Chtholly mercilessly argued, it was Chtholly who ended up running out of patience in the end.

Chtholly.

...A name echoed in her memories, one she never wanted to recall again. Something inside Nopht panged her. The two were the same age, but she was nonetheless Nopht's irritating senior, a friend she argued with often, and family she would never see again, all at once.

The anticipated day had already passed as they wasted time on the surface like this. An exceptionally large Six, Timere, would have launched its attack in the sky by then; Chtholly would have intercepted it and beat back their enemy in exchange for her life.

Just as planned, she would have thrown away her life in the anticipated battle. That was a leprechaun's duty. There was no need to be afraid, no necessity of feeling sad.

But when Nopht thought about how that cheeky and captious cerulean-haired girl would no longer be there once they finished this tedious work and returned to the sky, she felt a little empty.

"Nopht? What is it?"

"…It's nothing. If you say it's okay, Rhan, then I guess it's fine. Do what you want."

She threw herself backward onto the cot.

And as she did so, she nonchalantly turned her face away from the other two. She didn't want them to see her expression.

"I'm going to eat the whole meat pie."

"Just take half."

"Oh, very well, I suppose I will… Now, Glick, was it? You've been summoned here as an adviser—does that mean you've been salvaging for a long time?"

"Yeah, guess so. I'm confident I've been doing it longer than the guys who've only been around a short while."

"Then have you met a Beast before?"

Nopht shivered.

"Let's see…" Glick pressed his finger to his temple in a thinking pose. "I've been attacked by Two and Three and Six. If we count the ones I've seen from far away, I guess we can include Five and Eleven, too."

"That many?!"

Nopht pushed herself up. Her tears had evaporated.

"We've never fought anything else but Timere!"

"We're not fighting them head-on like you ladies are. Every time, we come home in shambles, barely holding on to our lives."

"—Yet it might be apt to think you are much more knowledgeable about the Beasts than we are."

"I wouldn't say I know enough to call myself knowledgeable. Oh, I get it. You want to ask me something about the Beasts, don't you, Blue Girl?"

"Yes…"

The paper crinkled as Rhantolk unwrapped the meat pie, her voice hushed.

"I always thought it was strange. It's been five hundred years since we were chased from the surface. We have lived thus far at the whims of the Seventeen Beasts. The miracle that we've managed to escape the looming jaws of the Beasts could even be called the very history of Regule Aire itself. Yet…we know much too little about what these 'Beasts' actually are."

Heeere we go again, Nopht thought.

Rhantolk was, at any rate, smarter than Nopht.

By smart, that meant she was used to the act of thinking itself and was skilled at finding topics to ponder. Or perhaps that meant she had to find an answer she was satisfied with for everything.

There should be no better solution to things that could not be solved by thinking about them than to not think about them.

"What *are* the Beasts anyway? Perhaps you don't mind if I ask your thoughts?"

She thought about things she didn't need to think about; she wanted to know things she didn't need to know.

Rhantolk's gaze pierced straight into Glick's amber-colored eyes.

2. The End of a Dream, the Beginning of a Dream

The warehouse lay deep in the forest on Regule Aire's Island No. 68.

On paper, it was a facility owned by the Winged Guard, a place where the Guard stored the valuable weapons in their possession. While that wasn't entirely false, it could scarcely be considered an accurate representation of the truth.

In that warehouse was a magnificent barracks, one that could easily house fifty people. Stored there—no, *living* there—were more than thirty very young girls. Incidentally, the Orlandry Merchants Alliance was paying for most of the maintenance management costs, and the actual caretakers of the facility were Orlandry employees; it was even designated on the map as "Orlandry Alliance Warehouse No. 4."

Morning came once again to the warehouse.

The intense light of daybreak asserted itself by illuminating the room through the curtains. The birds sang, their chirping loud and relentless.

Chtholly propped herself up in her bed and stared absently at the ceiling.

It felt like her memory had fogged over, and she had trouble recalling everything that happened up until the night before.

"Ngh…"

She rubbed her eyes with the backs of her hands lightly.

Her spine shivered, unprompted. Winter mornings were cold. She would get sick if she stayed in her pajamas for too long.

She wondered if she should get up.

Her mind still fuzzy, she tried to remember what her plans were for the day. But she couldn't. She felt like she remembered that there weren't any missions planned any time soon. Then that would mean after her daily training course, the rest of the day was free. That was nice. She wanted to use all the time she had, all the freedom she was allowed to follow after him.

—*Him.*

The image of a young man with black hair appeared in her mind's eye.

That was what spurred her vague memories of the night before to replay for her.

"…Whoa—"

Oh right—she had collapsed.

The encroachment from her past life had beaten her down, and she fell into a deep sleep she might not have ever woken up from. But for some reason, she did wake up, bursting into tears as she clung to Willem in front of everyone else, her stomach growling. She'd devoured the oatmeal that Lakhesh had so considerately brought to her, then was immediately overcome by extreme fatigue, and she slept hard.

"Uuuuugh…"

What was all that about?

Maybe that's what she was—a creature that operated only on her appetite and desire for sleep. Something that simply acted on instinct. Clinging to Willem with everyone present must have been one of her instincts, too. Where was her logic? There was a limit on how shameful something could be. Her face felt as if it would burst into flames.

But.

She felt a desire for food and sleep *because* she was alive. It was proof that her body was trying to continue on. When she considered that, she started to feel somewhat optimistic. No—from now on, she would convince herself to feel that way. Her spirit would wither away if she didn't.

She lightly smacked her burning cheeks and took a closer look at her surroundings.

This wasn't her room. This was the infirmary.

Someone must have carried her here after she suddenly lost consciousness in the hallway. Who that might have been was probably—no, *definitely*—Willem, but she wouldn't think too hard about it. A smile burst across her face.

Chtholly Nota Seniorious was the eldest of the faerie soldiers and a grown woman. She had to be a good role model for the little ones. Though she'd probably marred some of that image already, that was the very reason why she could not afford any more mistakes.

She decided to get up. She should splash some cold water on her face before someone saw her. Just as that thought crossed her mind and she placed her feet on the floor—

"Oh?"

The door opened, and there stood a redheaded woman.

"It looks like you're actually up now. What a relief."

She was tall and a bit older than Chtholly—probably around twenty. Though she was clearly an adult, her expression was somewhat childlike, and she wore a frilly blouse and apron to match.

"Willem was really worried, you know! He wondered if you were going to sleep for a long time again or if this time you weren't going to wake up. He insisted he stay by your side until you woke up, so I had to chase him out."

The woman kicked up the heels of her slippers as she entered the infirmary. She opened the curtains, changed the water in the flower vase, and changed the day on the calendar.

"Well, you were sleeping with such a nice smile on your face, and your pulse and breathing and other vital signs seemed okay, so I had you brought here to the infirmary for the time being. So how are you feeling?"

"Huh? Uh, um…"

For a moment, she couldn't understand that she was being asked a question.

She blinked.

"Nyggla…tho…?"

"Hmm?"

"Oh, uh, nothing."

She waved both her hands, flustered.

Right. This woman's name was Nygglatho. She had been dispatched by the Orlandry Merchants Alliance and held the high position of equipment manager here at the warehouse, and she also took care of the "equipment"—the young faeries.

"What's wrong? Are you still drowsy?"

"Yeah, I think so…"

Her head wasn't working as it should. It looked like the morning light and Willem's name were still not enough to wake up her mind, devoured by inactivity.

"I don't feel sick, but I feel blank. I think I'm going to wash my fac—"

"Miss Chtholly!"

The door that sat ajar burst fully open with a loud bang.

"You're not a ghost, Miss Chthollyyyyyy!"

A small green-haired girl dashed into the room like an arrow and clung to Chtholly.

"Bwuh?!"

"Come, now. Don't push Chtholly; she's just recovering from injury."

A small purple-haired girl peeked out from behind her.

"...Tiat. Pannibal."

She said their names, as though confirming who they were.

She stared down blankly at the back of the head of the girl who clung desperately to her stomach.

"I'm sorry, Miss Chtholly." Pannibal dropped her head. "Tiat was restless the entire time you were broken. I don't think she slept at all last night, ever since she saw you."

"Really?"

Now with an explanation, she asked Tiat for confirmation, but there was no answer.

She poked the girl, but there was no response.

Chtholly turned her over to check, and in that small time frame, she had fallen asleep.

"I see."

It seemed it was true that Tiat hadn't slept. The girl had worried so much about her, and that made her happy, or maybe it was heartwarming, or maybe she felt bad about it, or maybe it was precious, or maybe—

"You felt restless when you thought about someone dying, didn't you?"

—it made her a bit sad.

"You've grown up, Tiat."

They said that leprechauns were the result of babies' lost souls, who died before they understood what death was. That was why, strictly speaking, they were not "living" beings. And *that* was why their instinct to fear death didn't work. They didn't have the feelings to mourn someone else's death.

But that was when she was young.

As Chtholly grew into an older faerie, her feelings changed. Once her body matured and she began to walk the battlefield with sword in hand, she started to somewhat understand what death was. Her mind judged it to be an irreplaceable loss, something so sad and painful.

In terms of other races, that was considered growth. It was a good thing.

But for leprechauns, it was something terrible. They were beings born and raised to be spent on the battlefield. No one's spirit could handle it if one chose to mourn every single faerie who vanished. That was why many faeries pretended not to notice those feelings as they welled up inside them; they turned their gaze away. They rejected it as something they didn't need. They suppressed it as something they should overcome.

If Tiat had chosen to go with none of the above and instead face these unfamiliar feelings head-on, then there would surely be a rough future ahead of her.

"Don't be afraid to show how happy you are that she's matured."

Chtholly lifted her head in surprise. There was Nygglatho, smiling gently.

"Did I just say what I was thinking out loud?"

"No, but I understand how you feel. How long do you think I've been here, watching over you?"

…Oh, right.

How Chtholly felt about Tiat right now was the same as how her own seniors felt about her. And Nygglatho had always been right by their side, watching over them.

"Well, why don't we let Tiat sleep here in the infirmary for now? Chtholly, you…were going to wash your face, was it?"

"Oh yeah."

"Then when you're finished, come eat breakfast in the dining hall and show everyone that smile of yours. You can come back here when you're finished." Nygglatho pointed to the floor. "At first glance, you seem to be doing well, but we can't let our guard down just yet. What we can do with the equipment here may be limited, but we can provide you with a simple checkup."

"Oh…"

Right. That was important. Why hadn't she thought of that herself? Her brain still wasn't functioning. She had to wake up.

"Yeah, you're right."

Tiat was still sound asleep and clinging to her, but Chtholly peeled her off and laid her down on the bed. She lightly tapped herself on her cheeks to perk herself up.

"...Huh?" It was Pannibal, sounding confused. "Did you have a change of heart?"

"Huh?"

She pointed to Chtholly—specifically, a section of her hair.

Just in that portion of her cerulean hair, she found quite a few red strands.

"What...is this?"

She rubbed it, but the color stayed. She pulled on it, but it wasn't fake hair. She brought it up to the light coming from the window, but all that told her was that it was indeed her real hair color, not at all artificial.

"It must be an aftereffect of your previous coma. I don't think we have much to worry about. Hair color changes due to the weather or maturity aren't unusual in other races," Nygglatho chimed in. "It's a beautiful color. I think you should keep it as is; don't dye it back."

That was probably it.

Chtholly never really liked the color of her hair anyway, and she didn't mind at all if it ended up changing. Since only one part of her hair turned red, she didn't have to worry about the clothes she already had no longer matching. And—

"I'm sure Willem will say he likes you as you are, even if you don't force yourself to get all dolled up."

"Seriously, could you *not* read my mind, please?!"

Chtholly's protest sounded more like a whine.

†

What am I? Chtholly thought.

The answer sounded simple but was just a little bit complicated.

Leprechauns: the dead who failed to die. The living without life. Weapons who threw that all away for the sake of those who had real lives.

The name of her compatible dug weapon was Seniorious. She was fifteen years old. She was born in the forests of Island No. 94.

...And almost one month had passed since the emergence of her unrequited feelings.

3. I'm Home

Early in the morning, he went to the market to buy ingredients.

A cloth bag contained his spoils in one bundle: flour, butter, eggs, milk, sugar—and a little bit of honey, various nuts, and dried fruits.

Willem Kmetsch walked along a small forest path, the dappled sunlight filtering in through the trees.

The stones making the path were sparse and unkempt, various weeds breaking their way through the gaps. It wasn't exactly easy to traverse, but it at least kept them from getting lost as long as they followed it.

"Um, um, the bag isn't too heavy, is it?"

Lakhesh walked beside him, peeking up at him in concern.

"What do you take me for? I'm an adult. This thing's light as a feather." He readjusted the large bag he carried in his hands as he responded. "I might as well let you ride on my shoulders while I'm at it."

"O-oh, um, no thank you. I will pass." She hurriedly waved both her outstretched hands. "I, um, I know the way now because of work."

These girls—these faeries—were nominally secret weapons owned by the Guard, so their freedoms were heavily restricted. They were not allowed to leave the island to do anything if it was not a part of some battle strategy (though flying to nearby islands with their own wings was often tacitly permitted).

But on the other hand, they were guaranteed a rather free life here on Island No. 68.

"How long've you been working at the bakery?"

"Um, almost six months now. I made so many mistakes in the beginning, but now the manager has started to tell me I've been doing well."

"Huh."

A crabby middle-aged semifer man ran the bakery in the town center. It might have just been his natural expression, but he always looked grumpy and didn't seem the type to compliment others.

"He said he wants me to help make bread not only in the morning but also during lunchtime, and he said that he wished he could just adopt me."

"Huh."

"…U-um, Mr. Willem, is something wrong? You look scary."

It's nothing. I'm fine. I'm calm. I don't believe that blatant lip service at all. Yeah, I don't. That said, maybe I should go say hello to the baker sometime soon.

"Don't worry about it. I'm glad you got permission to take a part-time job. Soldiers aren't typically allowed to moonlight, y'know."

Strictly speaking, the faeries weren't soldiers but weapons. And no matter how he thought about it, any military allowing its weapons to take a side job wasn't normal… But then again, Willem himself was in the odd position of taking on a military role as a kind of side job. He wasn't in the position to really pursue the issue.

"I heard the important military man… The manager who worked here before you was real sour about it. But Miss Nygglatho convinced him."

"Oh… I see."

Nominally, these girls were weapons owned by the Guard. But in reality, they were private assets in possession of the Orlandry Merchants Alliance. Managers dispatched by the Guard were nothing but decoration, and the actual supervision was done by a caretaker dispatched by Orlandry. In this instance, that caretaker was Nygglatho. If she wanted to do something, the manager from the Guard would not be able to dispute it, whether they liked it or not.

"Oh… You're part of the military, too, right, Mr. Willem? Do you think this should be allowed?"

"Hmm?"

"Um, us as weapons of the Guard, working and saving money like anyone else…"

"Oh, that."

Sure, as someone clad in a Guard uniform, maybe he, too, should be making a sour face about it.

"Why not? If a kid says they found something they wanna do, then at the very least, it's the adult's job not to get in the way if they don't plan on supporting them. As long as you're not selling secret information or putting our equipment on the black market, I won't say no."

"Wow… Really?!" Lakhesh beamed. "Um, I love you so much, Mr. Willem! Us faeries don't have parents, so we don't really know what it's like, but if I had a dad, I'd want him to be someone like you."

"I love you so much." Huh.

They were words of affection, ones he was honestly happy about, ones he could readily accept.

"I'm already kind of like your parent."

"Really? Heh-heh-heh!"

Lakhesh grinned bashfully. Willem, in turn, smiled. But—

"…Oh, but then we need a mom… I love Miss Nygglatho, too, but I think Miss Chtholly would go better with you…"

Once she started murmuring about some terrifying-sounding things, he pretended not to notice, as always.

A baggy lab coat Chtholly had never seen before sat on Nygglatho's shoulders, over the apron she usually wore.

"I got this when I earned my basic medicine and cooking licenses at the academy."

She was a little surprised Nygglatho had something like that.

Medicine and cooking. Both of them were the most valuable skills someone working as the caretaker at the faerie barracks could have. And since she was a talented woman who had a good grasp on both, Nygglatho alone was left managing their home.

"I feel more motivated to do work wearing the lab coat, and we're going to make this checkup the real deal, okay?"

And then, just as she announced, she started a very authentic-seeming checkup.

She began with percussing and palpating all over Chtholly's body, then she brought a light to her eyes to see how they reacted. She had her take some medicine meant for the exam and asked how she felt, drew a little bit of blood, and made jokes such as, *"Oh, I think I would understand much more if I just had a nibble on your flesh."*

"Hmm..."

She took data, wrote them down on her chart, and took data again. As she repeated these actions, Nygglatho's expression became one that was hard to read, a mix of surprise and perplexity.

"I'm not infected with some kind of terrible disease or something, am I?" Chtholly asked doubtfully.

"Mm, no, that's not it. It really isn't, okay?"

She replied with an even more puzzling response.

The general checkup was over.

Nygglatho cradled her head with both her hands and lay face-first on the desk.

"...What does that mean? What happened?" Chtholly asked as she got herself dressed.

"The powdered purifying silver came back negative." Nygglatho sat up abruptly as she spoke.

"—And? What does that mean?" Chtholly asked nervously.

There was a myth that silver had the power to purify evil. Countless tales said that it could keep vampires away or cut short a troll's infinite life force.

But in reality, those were mostly nothing but tales.

Real silver was only a soft and unstable metal. It reacted readily with toxins and noxious gas, deteriorating and turning black. But at the same time, that meant it was a valuable tool in discovering those sorts of dangerous irregularities. That might have been why heavy and cumbersome silver utensils were popular among the rich—as a caution against poisoned food.

But it was hard to tell how this situation and that were related.

"Purifying silver is made with a special kind of ash that changes color not for regular poison and all that but in response to distorted death… To put it simply, it's a chemical meant for finding ghosts and ghouls and that sort."

"Ghosts…"

The word escaped Chtholly's lips absentmindedly.

She thought for a moment.

"Um… And what does that mean?"

She gulped hard, then asked another question.

"…Don't tell me that's *exactly* what you mean?"

"It is, of course. I have no idea what happened to cause this, but this is all I can say when I put together both conclusion and result." Nygglatho waved the test tube she held in her hand. The silver rattled around inside it. "As you know, leprechauns are a type of spirit. And so, by mixing your blood with the reagent, it should have turned black in an instant. But it was instead the impossible result of *no* reaction, so I can only come to one conclusion."

Her logic was clear and simple; there was absolutely no room to question it.

"In short, right now, you are not a leprechaun."

"…Wait. I don't follow. People are usually born as one race and stay that way until they die, right? You can't just decide one day, 'Hmm, I don't think I want to be a troll anymore,' then go down to city hall and start being something else the next day, right?"

"I don't know why you used trolls as your example, but generally, yes."

"Then, why?"

"I don't know why. I told you—it's just what it is by looking at both conclusion and result. I can't give you any further detail unless we take you to a specialist."

"But then I—"

The dug weapons—also known as Carillon—were superweapons that only the already-extinct emnetwiht could use. Leprechauns, who were beings born to work in place of the emnetwiht using their tools, however, could wield these ancient superweapons as though they were emnetwiht themselves.

That was the reason why the faeries had been placed in this warehouse as anti-Beast weapons.

"I know. It might be best for you not to come into direct contact with dug weapons anymore. We don't know what'll happen… I'm not threatening you! You know that if someone of any race not related to the emnetwiht touches a dug weapon, it might take a serious toll on their health, right?"

She knew. That was why the majority of the lizardfolk soldiers stayed away from them. The brave ones who interacted so closely with them, like Limeskin, made up only a small minority.

"You're featureless, and you don't look too different from an emnetwiht, but this isn't something we can decide by superficial features alone."

She knew that. The possibility was small, but it was there; she couldn't force her life into danger.

But.

She was named Chtholly Nota Seniorious because her compatible dug weapon was Seniorious. If she was no longer able to touch the sword, then all that was left was the worthless name of Chtholly.

"…If I can't use a sword, then I'm no longer qualified as a faerie soldier."

"That's true," Nygglatho casually agreed as she jotted something down at the bottom of the chart.

"And since I'm no longer a faerie soldier, I should leave."

"Um… I suppose that's the natural conclusion, isn't it?" The troll furrowed her brow. "Don't say that, though—you're staying here. I can take care of the one or two relevant documents for you to stay, and it's not like you have an active reason to leave now, right?"

"But—"

"*I have nothing to do here* is not a valid answer. You need to learn that the word *boredom* is not relevant to the life of a woman who has dreams and ambitions." She wagged her finger like a mother scolding a child. "You came home. And you are here now. You need to cherish this, you know."

"I know, but—"

"You're right. I suppose we can start your homemaking training in the meanwhile."

......

"What?"

"Seriously, though, Willem's contracted time here will be finished in three months. I mean, the job was originally one where the person in question could be gone, but we would make it seem like he was here on paper, so there's no basis for it at all if we decide to extend his contract. But to lose him after all this time would be a huge setback for us. Do you understand what I mean?"

She knew that. And yet...

"But this is Willem we're talking about, meaning if we asked him to stay, I doubt he would try to leave. That wouldn't be enough, though. He needs *something*—something tangible, something to make him truly feel like this is his home. Do you understand what I mean?"

She felt like she did, but at the same time, she didn't.

"You discipline the cows and sheep to come back to the barn at night if you want them to roam freely during the day, right?"

She didn't quite understand the metaphor.

"Not to mention that the emnetwiht bloodline has now been revived in the modern era—it would be such a pity to see it end with him alone. Even placing edibility aside, he should have a wife, start a family, and make children and grandchildren, no?"

Wait. Wait a second. Before she even considered if she understood this or not, she felt like it was something she wasn't supposed to understand.

"I was actually thinking that I might be a good candidate—"

"You can't!!"

Ka-thunk. Chtholly stood, kicking her chair backward, and it fell over with a loud clatter. Her face felt hot.

Nygglatho's shocked expression slowly transformed into a mischievous smile.

"I can't? Why?"

Willem himself had stated once before that he was into older, broad-minded women. Sadly, those were conditions Chtholly was incapable of fulfilling, no matter how hard she tried. And Nygglatho fulfilled them both perfectly, if only just those two things.

"...Then I won't...stand a chance."

"Really? I suppose that is where it's just a matter of opinion." Nygglatho shrugged slightly. "Then put your whole life into becoming a good woman and snatch him up. Some other girl or I might get ahead of you if you dilly-dally, you know." She chuckled as she spoke.

Chtholly now understood. That was what a broad-minded woman looked like.

She felt like all the things she lacked had been pointed out to her all over again.

✝

As the little ones headed for the field for their basic training course after breakfast, Willem took over the kitchen.

He put an apron over his Guard uniform, wrapped a kerchief around his head, and lined up on the table the big batch of ingredients he bought at the morning market.

And he baked a big butter cake.

Willem believed that the most valuable thing in battle was imagination. What were the exact conditions of the victory one had in mind? What sort of events could one suppose would happen just before and after those conditions were met? And what sort of conditions were necessary for the path leading to that goal? He believed only those who could prepare in their mind for every possibility were the ones who could make that future a reality.

As a veteran, he never let his guard down. He saw everything through this lens, for example: First, there was no questioning that the littlest faeries at the warehouse would want to eat the cake, too. Though he would try to reason with them, saying this was Chtholly's incentive and reward for coming home alive, it would still be difficult for all of them to accept it. But Chtholly was not the type to hog a whole cake to herself under such circumstances. She would most certainly want to let the other girls have some. And so, in order for Chtholly to have enough butter cake for herself, he had to bake at least some for other people.

So how did that turn out?

Once the day's basic training was finished and when the exhausted little faeries gathered in the dining hall, they squealed like animals. The hall was filled with a sweet scent, and sitting on the table was a large, freshly baked butter cake, steam faintly rising from it. Its lure was enough to blow all the reason out of excited little girls' minds.

Their eyes glinted like those of wild animals, and it looked as if puddles of drool would at any moment come dripping out of their slackened jaws.

Just as the girls, now transformed into hungry demons, were about to jump on the cake—

"We still keep our manners when we have a snack, remember?" said Nygglatho, the true hungry demon, smiling brightly.

The girls sat down quietly in their chairs, waited patiently until everyone else had received a slice, then after they said their before-meal prayers together, they all grabbed their forks and brought a bit of cake to their mouths at the same time, their eyes sparkling delightfully in unison.

Great, the first round of suppressive fire was a success; now, it was time to go straight into concentrating the bombardment onto Chth— But as he looked around the dining hall that was now filled with great energy, he realized the most important, cerulean-haired faerie was nowhere to be seen.

"Chtholly is probably in her room," Nephren told him as she munched on her cake, her eyes still glistening.

"Why? I thought I just told you to go get her."

"Well, y'know, she gets weirdly stubborn about stuff like this." Ithea, her chin resting in her palm, whirled around to look at him.

He'd heard about this before. Chtholly Nota Seniorious never ordered dessert when she ate in the faerie warehouse dining hall.

He thought she must not like sweet things, but on the contrary, it didn't seem like that was the case.

"That's because Miss Chtholly is a grown-up," Tiat had said proudly, as though she knew what was going on. She meant that it was childish to be excited by dessert, and it was adult women who said calmly, *"No, thank you."* That in itself was a pretty childish way of looking at things, but he wasn't going to say that out loud.

"She's too proud," Ithea had said with a playful smile. She was saying that she was putting on the boldest front she could muster as the oldest faerie in the warehouse, so that she may seem and act like the eldest and so that the younger ones might consider her reliable. And he thought that sounded a lot like something she would do.

And so, at any rate, none of the faeries who lived in this warehouse had ever seen Chtholly eat sweets.

"Well, it's not a big deal. You should hand deliver it to her room yourself, Officer, and spend some sweet, sweet time together."

"Don't be crude."

He poked Ithea's cheek.

Ten minutes later—Chtholly's room.

"...So how come you're the only one who didn't come to the dining hall? Even though you're the centerpiece of this whole thing?"

"Um, well, that's because... I don't really like the other girls watching me when I eat stuff like this..."

"Yeah, and *why*?"

"Because it's, y'know, kinda childish! Especially since I, um, apparently get really expressive when I eat this stuff. I just thought maybe I shouldn't act like that in front of the kids since I'm the oldest."

It was the very reasoning he'd gotten a grasp of and the very answer he was expecting.

Siiiiigh.

"Why are you sighing?"

"Just thinking about how you obsessing over little stuff like that makes you sound even more like a kid."

"Wha—?!"

Just as Chtholly was about to jump up from her chair, Willem placed a plate with a slice of cake before her.

It gave off a soft, sweet aroma.

The anger vanished from her eyes, and she immediately slumped back into her chair.

"Shall I pour some tea for you as well, young miss?" He chuckled as he placed a fork beside the plate.

"...Butter cake?"

"Yep." He didn't know why it had to be a question, but he nodded anyway.

"…There are nuts mixed into the batter?"

"Thought it might be a nice change for the flavor and consistency."

She took a good look at the cake slice from both sides.

"…It looks good."

"It *is* good."

"…I can eat this, right?"

"Of course. Who do you think I baked it for?"

He stared at her.

She lightly poked the fork into the cake.

Like chopping off the side of a mountain, she cut off a bite-size piece.

With a shaking hand, she brought it before her face.

"……"

She readied herself and put it in her mouth.

"All right, all right. Okay. I'll make you eat so much cake that you'll get heartburn."

He recalled the promises they made that night.

Now he was finally able to fulfill his.

And at the same time, this girl was finishing in his stead the things he was once unable to do. She returned from her battle to protect them. She came back to the place she belonged. And—

She came back to a warm *"Welcome home"* by those waiting for her.

Chtholly's mouth moved as she chewed. She made a slight sound as she swallowed.

"It tastes like butter cake."

"That's because it *is* butter cake," replied Willem, shrugging.

A large drop fell to Chtholly's knee with a *plop*.

"I know… I know this is late, but… I really…I really did make it home, didn't I…?"

It had almost been ten full days since Chtholly and the two other faeries returned to the warehouse. It had been over two weeks if he counted the time since the battle itself had ended.

And yet it was only now that this girl had fully grasped that truth.

Willem never saw the battlefield on Island No. 15 with his own eyes.

And so he did not understand how heavily this promise had weighed on Chtholly. He had no idea, meaning all he could do was guess.

"You did well."

All he could do was toss some trite, sympathetic words her way with a dumb look on his face.

"Yeah… I… I did really well…" The tears spilling from her eyes quickly dampened her sleeves. "I'm sorry… I… I don't know how it tastes anymore… I think it's probably good, but…I can't think of any other words…"

"I see."

Chtholly's shoulders quivered. Willem sat beside her, thinking.

What would have happened if he were in her position?

Basically—well, of course it was entirely impossible—had he been able to keep the promise he'd made with Almaria, what would've happened? Had he protected what he wanted to, gone home to the place he wanted to, then eaten his fill of her exquisite butter cake as proof of that, then what would he have done?

He probably would have cried his eyes out without a worry for shame.

He probably would have rained a relentless hurricane of hugs and kisses on all the kids in the orphanage. They all probably would have called him annoying or too forceful or gross and tried to push him away, but he still would have never let them go.

"There's more if you want some. You can stuff your face to your heart's content, okay?"

"Yeah…I know. I know, but my heart just feels so full."

She hadn't had much more than two bites.

Oh well. Willem smiled wryly and lightly patted the top of her head.

She didn't yell at him for treating her like a child.

"I said it yesterday, and it really is kind of late, but— Welcome home, Chtholly."

"Oh…"

The fork slipped from her hand.

After a few hiccups, Chtholly slowly raised her head.

Her deep cerulean eyes were overflowing with tears.

"I'm...home..."

Chtholly pushed her forehead onto Willem's stomach.

He could feel how hot her tears were through the fabric of his Guard uniform.

"I said it..."

"Yeah, you did. And I finally heard it."

He lightly patted the back of her head.

Chtholly sobbed as she clung to Willem, her body shivering in what must have been more than simple happiness.

4. Warm Days in a Cold Season

He'd heard that the end of the hallway on the second floor was leaking recently.

When he went to go see for himself, he saw how it might need a little handiwork. Since they'd have to call in someone from town later for proper repairs, all he had to do now was just some emergency patching up—

"...Hmm?"

Willem, staring at the ceiling, tilted his head.

"What is it? Did you see something off?"

Chtholly traced his gaze, but she didn't spot anything particularly odd. The weathered old ceiling boards were darkened, as they always were.

"No, I just felt like something like this happened before."

"Really?"

He recounted his memories.

"____"

He couldn't pick out any specific one that was like this.

"I think the last thing you repaired was a wall that Collon kicked in."

"That's not exactly what I mean, but… Eh, whatever. If I can't remember, then it means it probably wasn't important." Willem tilted his neck to either side, cracking it. "Yup, the boards and nails I used last time are still here… Hey, you know where the hammer is?"

"Didn't you ask me that before? Did you forget already?"

Now that Chtholly mentioned it, Willem thought she was probably right.

"Oh, sorry 'bout that. You know where they are?"

Chtholly said with a smile, "What are we going to do with you?" She opened her mouth to say something—

"_____"

"…Huh?"

There was no doubt in her mind that she should know where the hammer was. So then why couldn't she think of where it might be?

"What's up?"

"I'm sorry, um, uh…I think…I forgot, too?"

"What, you too? We sure got ourselves a slippery hammer."

"Y-yeah…" Chtholly nodded hesitantly.

She felt a faint chill, but she told herself it wasn't a big deal.

"Well, we probably don't need to worry too much about it. Since we both forgot, all we need to do is just ask some unrelated third party, yeah?"

"Yeah…yeah, you're right."

Willem was kind. He wasn't exactly awkward in the way he treated the girls. It was more that sometimes he had no idea what he was supposed to do; yet when he stayed near them, it was always clear he was doing his best to be considerate of them. She could feel it.

And that made her want to stay by him. She wanted to snuggle up close to him. She wanted to fawn on him.

She forced herself to smile.

"Let's go. It's probably in one of the supply closets either here or downstairs."

"Yeah, okay."

Willem turned around and walked off.

Chtholly stared at his empty left hand. Would he be surprised if she ran up to his side and grasped it? She…didn't think he would refuse, but would it give him a good impression?

Now that she thought about it, she remembered when Nephren was hugging his arm on Island No. 11, and while he didn't resist, he did seem a bit troubled by that. She hated the idea that he might make the same face if she held his hand.

She started to walk, half a step behind him, still worrying about it.

"Wooooooow…"

Tiat, peeking only half her face out from the corner of the hallway to watch, grew excited.

"They're so much like grown-ups…"

Lakhesh, also peeking only half her face out from the same corner, flushed red.

"Well, y'know what it means when she's a half step behind him. They're not acting reserved or anything; they just don't know how to close the distance between them when they're alone."

Ithea, doing the same as the other two, was astonished.

"I can hear everything you're saying!"

Chtholly called out to them in a loud voice, and all three of the stacked faces slipped back behind the wall.

†

Five days had passed since she woke up.

There didn't seem to be any visible problems with Chtholly's physical health for the time being.

Though she hadn't exactly decided to go with Nygglatho's suggestion, there was nothing else for her to do now that she could no longer fulfill the role of a faerie soldier. She took the time she used to fill with her own training and all that and went straight into investing it in other things. Namely, instructing the younger faeries in their training, helping Nygglatho, and whatnot.

✝

She scooped some of the soup in the ladle and gave it a taste. She could feel it tingle the tip of her tongue. It wasn't bad. But when she considered how rich it would get after she added the mutton to it, she thought that maybe a sharper taste would be better.

She chopped some herbs and sprinkled them into the pot.

"…Another meat dish with lots of spices? Sounds like a favorite of *someone* I know."

Ithea sniffed the air as she spoke. But Chtholly kicked her out, her reason being, "No one is allowed in the kitchen besides the day's cook!" Incidentally, this rule applied only to the faeries, so Nygglatho and Willem, and now Chtholly (acting as Nygglatho's assistant), could use the kitchen as they liked.

The veggies that would go along with the soup should probably be boiled to be a bit sweeter. At the very least, the little faeries would like that better, but she did not quite have enough information to judge if it suited the tastes of the man in question or not.

Well, there wasn't much she could do about it. She would just make it as an experiment for today, then serve it as is during mealtime and see what his reaction was. Better today than tomorrow. Better tomorrow than the day after. As long as she kept maturing like this, she would one day become the person she wanted to be.

"I don't think it's fair you get to hog the kitchen all to yourself just so you can capture some guy's heart and stomach!"

She heard the yell coming from just outside the kitchen, so she threw the ladle to chase her away.

✝

The girls ran.

They'd heard that they would be able to see some comets in the northern sky.

The weather was nice that day; the air felt crisp. There was no way they could miss even more color in an otherwise already clear, starry sky.

The question was where they should be to watch them. From the big window in the dining hall? From the windows in the children's rooms? From the bench in front of the main entrance? No, no, watching the sky in such boring spots was of no importance. They had the *best* front-row seats.

The faerie warehouse sported a roof. Large amounts of laundry fluttered on it during the day, and at night, it could serve as the premier observation deck.

The girls dashed about restlessly. They shoved past one another as they made their way down the hallway, each fighting for the best spot to be enwrapped in the stars. Then—

"Hold! It! Right! Theeere!"

Tiat yelled, running after them with a towel in hand.

"We're supposed to dry our hair right after getting out of the bath! Otherwise we're gonna get sick!"

She was right. It was the truth. But kids acted with little regard for what was right or true whenever something caught their interest. That was especially the case for young faeries, who paid no heed to their own well-being.

The girls ran, their wet hair streaming behind them. Beads of water flew everywhere. Tiat followed behind.

"I! Told! You! To! Waaait!"

She grabbed on to one, pulled a bath towel over her, and began to scrub her catch's head vigorously. But the other girls simply kept on running. Tiat would never be able to catch them all.

They could hear Tiat struggling from the outside of the warehouse.

"She's really acting like the big girl she needs to be, huh?" Willem expressed his admiration as he sat on the bench, gazing up at the night sky. Tiat was still around ten years old, still on the short side, with limbs to match; plus, her thoughts and actions were still childish. He thought it was a bit unexpected—and Chtholly did, as well—that the little Tiat was acting like one of the older girls.

But it wasn't enough to surprise him. He saw through the tricks.

"I think she's copying me." Chtholly chuckled. "I was chasing those girls around like that not too long ago."

"I see. Now I get it."

Still gazing up at the sky, Willem's eyes drooped gently.

Chtholly also looked up to the same sky and then quickly stole a glance at Willem's profile. For now, he seemed perfectly relaxed. Chtholly's heart was pounding rather noisily from sitting beside him on the same bench, but that didn't seem to be the case for this man. She felt strange—slightly resentful but, at the same time, comfortable as they were.

"Oh yeah, that's what it was like when I first met you. Man, I know it wasn't long enough ago to feel nostalgic about it, but you know what I mean?"

"Huh…?"

—End
less gla
ss bea
ds fall
ing down.

"Oh yeah, never got to ask, did I? Why were you on Island No. 28 back then anyway?"

…

"You *really* need to be invested in Market Medley and stuff like that to visit it for sightseeing. I guess you were fighting a Beast or something nearby and stopped off on your way home, huh?"

……

"The buildings there are all jumbled together this way and that, and it's not very safe, either, so all sorts of nasty stuff ends up falling from the sky. It's usually kettles and oil cans, but sometimes it's a chicken, which is a big help with dinner."

.... *What?*

"But that was my first time seeing a girl fall from the sky. I was pretty surprised."

.... *What is he talking about?*

She didn't know this story. Though she could imagine it must have been some sort of precious memory, she couldn't find it within her own memories. She hadn't forgotten. And it wasn't missing.

The girl she thought she knew she was, was no longer there.

"...Chtholly? You okay?"

"Ah... Um..."

She didn't know how to answer.

She wasn't confident she could accurately describe the odd feeling that was running through her mind if she tried to put it into words. No, she was more afraid of disillusioning Willem if she did. She was terrified that he would realize she was not worth holding dear with the way she was now.

"I, uh..."

What was that?

What had she been thinking about?

Willem was worrying about her. She had to look up at him and say she was okay. She needed him to stop worrying. She couldn't have him suspect her. She couldn't have him realize something was off. She couldn't let him know the truth. What was off? What was the truth? She didn't know. She didn't know, but it was important. That was a line she couldn't cross if she wanted to stay Chtholly Nota Seniorious.

"Hey."

Willem peered down at her dubiously.

Ding.

There came an ominous metallic sound from above them.

She looked up instinctively.

The outside of the warehouse roof was surrounded by a metal rail. But not only was it not a particularly nice-looking rail, it was deteriorating and rickety, and there was the dangerous possibility of it breaking under just the slightest weight. Everyone had been pretty busy recently, and they kept putting off fixing it sooner rather than later.

They spotted a little girl at second-floor height, having just fallen into the air from the roof. She was especially small, even among all the little faeries. Her hair was a messy lemon-yellow.

(Almita?!)

She wasn't that high up, but on the other hand, it wouldn't take long until she hit the ground. If they ran from where they were, they would not make it in time.

Willem dashed off.

He didn't use that speedy something-sweep technique. It was too far of a distance. A skill developed especially for traversing short distances quickly could not be used for anything just a bit farther than its limits. But there was no way he could make it in time on his flesh-and-blood leg strength alone.

Chtholly used her Sight.

She could see the magic beginning to fire up inside Willem.

(Urgh, that idiot—!!)

She kicked off the ground.

Willem's body was covered in old wounds, to the point where Nygglatho had even commented, *"It's strange how you're alive."* For him to activate his venenum with a body like that was suicide. And this man was going to commit suicide with a straight face in order to keep his precious girls safe.

So she activated her own magic first.

She spread out her phantasmal wings, a blue-silver phosphorescence scattering around her, gliding through the air at about waist height. She surpassed Willem as he ran, twisted her body around to face the sky, and spread out her arms; she caught the girl's body in her bosom just as the girl was about to hit the ground and curled around her.

Chtholly crashed to the ground.

Impact.

But a body in motion does not stop so easily. She hit the ground countless times, tumbling as she did so, and finally stopped when she hit the wall of the faerie warehouse.

"...Phew."

She wasn't going to say she wasn't in pain. But her activated venenum had protected her body, and she couldn't spot any obvious wounds. The girl in her arms looked to be in a daze but seemed fine otherwise.

"Chtholly?!"

Willem rushed over to her, his voice strained.

"Sheesh... You sound like you're about to cry. Aren't you an adult?" She stood up and brushed off the dirt that clung to her shoulders and the hem of her clothes. "I'm fine. See? Almi... Um"—she gently rocked the girl in her arms—"the girl is fine. She got a little dirty, though."

"That's not the problem here! You overdid it! Are you dizzy?! Can you feel your fingers?! No weird sensations running down your spine?!"

He grabbed her shoulders and pressed closer.

"H-hey, you're too close! I appreciate it, but this is wrong! Try it again!"

"Listen! Magic is a contradiction to our life force. Activating it is just the same as abandoning the very energy that's keeping you alive. You can't call yourself a sorcerer without a mechanism to step in just before you die!"

Of course she knew that.

That was the first step of first steps, most basic of basic logic for anyone who consciously used magic.

"And a leprechaun's strength to live is scant in the first place. So even without a restriction on your life force, the magic you can create is incredibly strong."

"Yeah, so—"

"That was *different*!" he yelled, his voice pained. "What the hell was up with the way you activated it? It was so reckless! Leprechaun or not, you'd normally be dead the moment you did that!"

"Oh..."

Now that he mentioned it, he was right. It was the first time she realized that.

Activating venenum was like kindling a fire. One needed to spend time carefully handling a smaller flame to raise it in order to wield the power of a roaring blaze. It was not meant for responding to spur-of-the-moment situations. At the very least, it shouldn't be.

It wasn't enough to be reckless or dangerous.

Logically speaking, there was no way she should have been able to pull that off.

"I… I thought…I was going…to lose you…again…"

"Oh geez."

Her head had been feeling funny for the past while, and she had a lot to think about, and Willem's face was too close to hers, and looking at him like this, she realized how long his eyelashes were, and she started noticing other stuff like that, and she was starting to hate it.

"Calm down."

She lightly smacked his cheek.

And she smacked her own while she was at it. She, too, needed to calm down.

"First, I need to say the same thing to you. If I hadn't done it, you would've done it first. That thing where you force your magic to activate and run really fast. I was watching, okay? I could see it."

Willem's breath caught in his throat.

"And I'm fine. I'm not dizzy, and my spine feels okay. My fingers feel a bit tingly, but it's not like I can't move them at all. It'll get better pretty quickly."

"You're not putting up a front, are you?"

"Don't you believe me? Sheesh."

She grinned and removed herself from Willem's grip on her shoulders.

She looked up to the roof. Just as she suspected, the railing was completely broken. Tiat was on her hands and knees beside it, looking down at them, her eyes brimming with tears.

"It's okay—I caught her!" Chtholly waved up to her, and Tiat beamed. "But it's still dangerous up there, so no one is allowed on the roof for now! Take all the children there back downstairs!"

"O-okay!"

Tiat scrambled to her feet and corralled the group of children still on the roof. Chtholly figured she probably didn't need any help with that.

"Well then, I'm going to draw this girl a bath. You go help Tiat."

"Oh… Okay…" Willem nodded, perplexed.

Luckily, there was still plenty of warm water left in the washtub. There was no need to gather more from the river or use venenum to boil it again.

And so, just as Chtholly said she would, she put the girl into the bath.

She massaged the foamy liquid soap into her frizzy, lemon-yellow hair.

Her thin, fluffy locks had gotten mangled with quite a bit of dirt from rolling on the ground. Chtholly had to wash it thoroughly.

"Uh, um…" The girl, her eyes squeezed shut, hesitantly began to speak. "I'm…sorry."

"…You should be apologizing to Tiat, not to me. If you'd have listened to what she said, this wouldn't have ended up so serious."

"O-okay… I'm sorry."

Is she even listening to me?

That was what she was thinking, but there wasn't much she could do about it. It was typical for girls Almita's age to lose track of what they did once they shrank away from the reality that they'd done something worth reprimanding. And since the girl felt no fear for having almost lost her life in the first place, she probably had no idea *why* everyone else was so angry with her like this.

Every living being had a natural instinct to survive. Yet leprechauns lacked that and were still alive. Chtholly thought again how odd it was.

She suddenly looked up.

There was a large mirror in the bathroom at the faerie warehouse. When Nygglatho first came to the warehouse, it was one of the things she installed, insisting, *"Whether weapons or not, young girls should always look their best!"* There were plenty of other things that were added when she came, but those were for another time.

"…Hmm?"

Something was strange about her reflection in the mirror.

Red.

Something was red. It was her hair. It was just yesterday…no, just a few hours ago that only a small section of her hair was red, but at some point, it had spread to almost a third of her head.

What was going on?

Nygglatho mentioned that some semifer races changed color as the seasons changed or as they matured, but Chtholly felt like this situation was a bit different. Their hair would fall out and grow back a different color, not change color while it was still attached to their bodies like this. So really, whatever was happening to her was something completely diffe—

The girl with
the red
eyes
is looking this
way.

This feeling…

Images, both absurd and unknown, flashed before her eyes.

That's right. She remembered now. She looked like someone who wasn't her. She felt a baseless hatred and a sense of loss, and—

"…Elq…?"

She remembered the name.

She remembered nothing but the name.

"Wha…? What…is…?"

Her body shook. Her eyes spun.

"Chtholly?" The little girl, her head still covered in bubbles, turned back dubiously and looked up at her. What was this girl's name again? She didn't know. Was she supposed to know? She was one of the thirty-some residents here in the faerie warehouse; she was supposed to be a precious member of her family. Why? How?

"Are you cold?"

No. She wasn't cold. Something else entirely was freezing her heart from the inside. But she didn't know what it was. She couldn't put it into words.

✝

She wanted to hear her warm welcome home.

She wanted to announce her return.

She wanted to eat butter cake.

All her wishes came true.

She came home to the place she was meant to be. She saw the man she wanted to see so dearly. She had done everything she wanted to do. And so—

She was out of promises.

The end that had been shadowing her silently placed its hand on her shoulder.

Even Without a Visible Future
-moonlit sorcery-

1. The Girl Without a Face

What am I? Chtholly thought.

She was Chtholly Nota Seniorious. Mature faerie soldier. Compatible wielder of dug weapon Seniorious. Someone who had met the single living emnetwiht, Willem Kmetsch, and received from him his teachings—as well as hope.

Really?
...Really.

†

She summoned Ithea in the middle of the night.

"Brrr, sure is cold. Shoulda worn another layer."

They sat at the top of a small hill next to the aire-port. It was always windy here. It gave them a good vantage point, so they'd know right away if someone was coming.

"Sorry. This shouldn't take too long, so bear with me."

"...Hmm?"

Ithea shivered, then narrowed her eyes to study Chtholly.

"So's that why you brought me all the way out here? For a little chat? You got something you don't wanna risk someone else overhearing?"

"Yeah, something like that. But you should already know what I'm here to talk about, shouldn't you?"

"Hey, come on. I just know a little more and hear a little more than your average person, but I'm not a god. It's not like I know anything and everything." She placed the lantern on the ground as she spoke and sat herself down as well. "Actually, there's something I want to check with you, too. If ya don't mind, I'd prefer if I asked you my questions first."

"...Okay, sure. What are they?"

"Who are you?"

She asked it so naturally, almost as though she was asking what was on the menu for dinner that night.

Chtholly's breath caught for a second.

"Chtholly Nota Seniorious."

After a quick, deep breath, she slowly stated her own name, biting into her words.

"You sure?"

"Do I look like anyone else?"

"Guess you have a point."

The wind teased Chtholly's hair.

Her blue hair melted into the darkness of night and rendered it practically invisible. But the red mixed in stood out from the rest, and it looked like it was dancing in the wind.

"...Okay then, all the questions from me are done. Your turn."

"Mm."

She looked up to the sky. The black clouds looked like nothing more than shadows, and they sped across the sky above her with fantastic speed. Beyond them, she spotted the blurry stars and a somber gold-colored moon.

"I was really worrying about how I should talk to you about this, but if you're asking me questions like that, then I guess it's safe to say you've seen through me, right?"

"Not really. That was more like a surprise question to force an answer out of you, in the style of our officer, and there's only one thing I can confidently say I got from that: Your past-life encroachment hasn't gone away or stopped. The personality and memories of Chtholly Nota Seniorious are—in the present continuous tense—being taken over. Right?"

"Yeah. I think so." She grabbed her hair as it whipped about violently and held it to her chest. "Past-life encroachment itself is already rare, and for it to happen before the twenty-year mark is irregular in an already rare case... Right? Is this how your encroachment progressed for you, too?"

"I guess you could say so. I myself don't really remember much, and I think the process was a lot different compared to yours."

Ithea gave a sloppy grin.

The smile was a mask. Whenever this girl tried to hide how she was really feeling, she would always plaster on this vague smile.

"We've known each other a long time, and you knew the *old Ithea*, too, right? She was bright, nosy, got so involved in everything around her it was annoying, and yet wasn't honest at all—loved creating fiction and never went a day without writing in her diary. That's what Ithea Myse Valgulious was like. I first learned that when I read through the girl's entire diary."

Ah, right, I remember, thought Chtholly.

It was about two years ago. There was a time just after Ithea became an adult faerie soldier when she said she'd caught a cold and spent days holed up in her room. This girl must have spent all those days urgently reading through the many, many diaries.

In hindsight, now that she thought about it, it was about that time when Ithea's personality changed slightly... But maybe, maybe not. Back then, they weren't close enough friends to talk about that.

"Was it hard?"

"Sure. I thought I was gonna go crazy. There were so many times I just wanted to die. But if I did that, it wasn't like the original owner of this body...the real Ithea...was going to come back.

"I guess the only way I could pay for my sins was to inherit the life of the poor child I erased, of Ithea Myse Valgulious, without anyone noticing... Well, that's what I told myself, at least, and I've made it this far."

"We're being tricked, aren't we?"

"Yeah. Does that make you mad?"

Did it? Was she angry?

Chtholly asked herself. She felt no anger, no bewilderment. There was just an oddly silent feeling of understanding.

"A diary, hmm." She sat down by "Ithea's" side. "Maybe I should start one."

"I dunno. I feel like in your case, it'd be impossible to pass on your life without anyone noticing. Unlike me, see, your appearance is changing."

Oh, right.

Maybe the red mixed into her hair would eventually completely overtake her own blue. It wouldn't be easy to deceive the doubtful gazes around her with such an obvious change present.

"Who is it you want to pass on your life to, Chtholly? I know you probably don't want to hear this from me, but someone who's not you is going to be going to all the places you wanted to go, and it's going to be someone else settling down in the places you wanted to stay, you know."

Oh no. She certainly didn't like the sound of that.

"All your feelings of wanting to go somewhere and the wishes you have of staying there will quickly disappear. Regret won't help anything."

She hugged her knees tightly.

"...Or maybe I should die now, while I still remember things."

"That's one choice you have. I'm serious. We live clinging to our hearts and souls, but you're going to lose that foundation entirely. It'll be a lot harder than you can imagine."

"Yeah..."

She buried her face in her knees.

The girl sitting beside her wrapped her arms around her shoulders.

"What's wrong, Ithea?"

"The wind is strong, and I'm cold. I've got low body temp, and I'm not like Nephren, so please forgive me."

"...Ah-ha." A small laugh naturally spilled forth. "Thanks for the chat. You're pretty warm, though."

"Great. It was worth it living till today then, huh."

So that's what it was.

She didn't know if it was a phenomenon that was happening as a result of a series of coincidences or if it was happening because someone else intended it to. But past-life encroachment was, in the end, real encroachment—even possibly an invasion.

Her self would be undermined, her heart broken, her memories pruned, her spirit killed...and her past life's spirit, revived through the process of being remembered, would come back and snatch up the physical body she left behind. And none of that had anything to do with her past life's wishes at all—it all progressed and concluded automatically.

There was no miracle of love here.

Even if there was, time would soon be running out.

The girl named Chtholly Nota Seniorious would soon disappear.

"You keeping it a secret from the officer, then?"

"Yeah. He'd get worried if he found out about this."

"Well, why not make him worry? You've got that right, y'know."

"Yeah, maybe."

It wasn't that she hadn't thought about it. But if she told him, then she would end up spending the very little time she had left looking at his strained expression.

She wanted him to think fondly of her.

But she didn't want him to cry for her.

It wasn't like she wanted him to look at her as someone with the added value of being a tragic heroine.

"I want to be happy just a little longer. And I want him to be happy, too... I guess."

"Uh-huh," the girl said, a hint of annoyance in her voice. "That annoying *I'm so in love!* appeal of yours tells me you're still no one else but Chtholly, at least."

"*That's* how you can tell? Sheesh."

The two exchanged glances and smiled sadly at each other.

"At the very least, under no circumstances should you use your magic," the girl beside her spoke with an absent voice. "Of course, I am me, and you are you. Faeries are, no doubt, a result of a fantasy. The literal only thing they have in common with one another is being the product of souls of children who died too young. Both you and I are the same race but, at the same time, completely different. It doesn't mean we operate under the same logic. But still, I have this much advice for you."

"Okay." Chtholly nodded.

"You must absolutely never touch a dug weapon. If you want to stick around any longer, that's the least you can do."

"Okay... I won't. Thank you, Ithea."

"By the way, you haven't asked what my real name is, right? Or who I really am?"

Chtholly had thought it would be a strange thing to ask.

"You're Ithea, *too*, aren't you? You're bright, nosy, get so involved in everything around you it's annoying, and yet not honest at all." She lightly poked Ithea's nose with the tip of her finger. "You're an important colleague of ours—a friend. You don't look like anyone else to me."

"Ba-ha-ha-ha, I appreciate it."

She couldn't trust Ithea's smile. Almost everyone who lived in the faerie warehouse felt the same way. No one could entirely believe the expressions of someone who, whether she was happy or sad, angry or perplexed, was always smiling.

But.

Chtholly thought it was probably okay to trust her. It was a little different this time.

A teardrop sat at the corner of Ithea's eye, glinting slightly as it reflected the lantern's wavering light.

2. A Girl's Crush and a Woman in Love

He had a terrible dream.

In his dream, the master, Navrutri, and His Majesty the Emperor all sat together, drinking.

All three of them were extreme in their treatment of women, each in different ways. And so, of course, they seasoned their drinks with talk of women.

The master, who was nothing but an old pervert, spoke candidly about boobs and butts; Navrutri, who claimed he had lovers in every city he visited (which was probably true), retold his memories of a beautiful woman he met in the Sands Federation; the Emperor, known for playing around with all his ladies-in-waiting (and for being a henpecked husband), mentioned the innocence of one of the new maids, his eyes hazy like those of a teenage boy in a daydream.

I don't want anything to do with this.

The second that thought crossed his mind, the three reached out to grab his shoulder.

"Let's hear your story, too," Navrutri said, his voice needlessly sweet.

"I know you have things to confess," the master said, pressuring him with a sickening smile.

"Oh, I do believe I heard you were spending some time alone with my niece the other day," the Emperor said, pressuring him about something outrageous.

"Wait, I have my daily training to go to right now—" He tried to run, but he couldn't. They pinned him down and poured glass after glass of alcohol down his throat, and his consciousness soon went hazy, his mouth began to move on its own, and he started to name the names of all the girls around—

"—Officer. Hello, Officer! Why're you sleeping here?"

He heard a voice, and Second Officer Willem Kmetsch awoke.

He spun his head around, getting his bearings.

The first thing he noticed was a huge, unorganized stack of paper. The next thing he saw was a huge, unorganized stack of paper. To his right and left and above him and below him, no matter where he looked, all he could see were the same things.

To put it simply, this was the material room.

"You weren't in your room, so I was wondering where you might be, but here you are! Of all places."

"...Oh, Ithea."

The girl with straw-colored hair planted her hands on her hips in frustration.

"Yeees, 'tis me, Ithea Myse Valgulious, at your service. By the way, if you don't head to the dining hall now, there won't be any breakfast later."

"Oh..."

For the first time in a while, he wanted to tidy up the room.

But sure enough, the troubles in this vast voyage mounted one after the other, and he completely lost track of when he should take a break, much less what sort of information he should be fishing for. Then, before he knew it, he'd fallen asleep on the couch.

"I wouldn't want to miss a meal, that's for sure."

He stood up.

A small girl rolled off the sofa.

"...Ow."

A girl with ashen-colored hair sat up as she complained disinterestedly.

"Oh, I *thought* it was pretty warm. So you were my blanket, Nephren."

"Yes. It's cold out now, and I don't want you getting sick."

That made a lot of sense, and he honestly appreciated it.

"Thanks... And why are you sleeping here, too?"

"Well. It's cold out now, and I don't want to get sick."

But that didn't make much sense, and he probably shouldn't take it at face value.

"Collon came down with a fever yesterday, and she's been sleeping ever since, and both Tiat and Almita have started sneezing. I think we've come to the season where if we're not careful, we'll catch it, too."

"I appreciate the consideration, but if you're gonna sleep anywhere, sleep in your own room." He lightly poked her forehead.

Ithea watched the exchange quietly, her eyelids drooping to the point that they were almost closed.

"This would look super inappropriate if I saw this out of context, so why doesn't it look that way?"

"It's 'cause your mind hasn't been totally tainted yet, that's why."

Ithea tilted her head as if to say, *"Should I be happy about that?"*
"Nephren," she added. "He's pretty much just treating you like a pet. Are
you okay with that?"

"Emotional support is important. I believe it's a worthwhile responsibility."

"I see."

Now that honestly made sense.

"...C'mon, let's go get some breakfast."

Nephren sleepily rubbed her eyes, and Willem pulled her up.

"Oh, right— Officer, how's Chtholly doing?"

"What do you mean by *how*?"

"I was just wondering how she felt after being on the receiving end of
such passionate charm. I guess she's not as unhappy as we thought, then?"

"I'm not gonna say no, but it's none of your business."

"Oh." She looked surprised. "So you do have some heart for her?"

"My heart's been pounding from the start. I'm not a crusty old man
or some pervert with peculiar interests. You think there's some young guy
out there who won't get excited when a cute girl likes him? But I still can't
accept her, so I'm trying my hardest to throw her off, y'know?"

"Huh."

...What the hell was he talking about?

His mouth was running off in strange directions thanks to the weird
dream he had. He sensed going any further would be dangerous territory,
so he clammed up.

"Don't tell her" was all he added with a groan.

†

"You were sleeping with Nephren?!"

The question came as he was walking down the hall, and someone suddenly grabbed his ear.

He gritted his teeth through the pain and turned around, and standing
there was a girl with cerulean—no, cerulean *and* red hair. Chtholly wore a

visibly cross expression and looked up at him with wide, angry eyes, glaring sharply into his own.

It was somehow honestly frightening.

"Sheesh, you too?"

He tapped the hand that was holding his ear, urging her to let go.

"Can you not say it like that for everyone to hear? What's wrong with an adult and a child snoozing happily under the same blanket?"

"You're not older by enough years to be considered an adult."

"Ha! I know I look young, but y'know I was actually born over five hundred years ago, right?"

"I know. *And* I've heard you spent most of those five hundred years sleeping. That excuse isn't effective enough for you to look at me with that *gotcha!* face of yours."

Urgh. Really? He was a bit shocked precisely because he felt so confident.

"Well, I can't imagine you were the one who invited her in, so I think that Nephren probably crawled in on her own."

That was obvious.

"But I still don't get it. You were so confident you'd avoided so many bloodbaths in the past, right? So why didn't you notice when she came right up to you? Why'd you tell me you could avoid being stabbed in your sleep?"

"They're two completely different things. All I can sniff out are enemies. I'm not gonna be wary of people who aren't hostile to me—come on."

"Then let me ask you this—if that was Nygglatho, what would you have done?"

"Thrown her out the window in two seconds," he responded quickly and confidently.

That was the obvious choice. Letting a troll—and one who had previously declared her appetite for him with gusto, at that—get up close and personal with him would be like asking for certain death.

"See? You'd treat her differently than you did Nephren."

"No wait you can't talk about them like they're the same because even if there's no hostility I'll still respond if there's danger sheesh I don't want to die okay and even if that troll isn't hostile she still has this like general aggressiveness so I really need to be aware of that okay?"

"You sound suspicious when you talk fast like that."

"…What do you want me to do?" He dropped his shoulders, disheartened.

"Then let me ask you another thing. What would you have done if it was me?"

"Of course—" He thought for a moment. He was sure things would get more complicated if he gave a careless answer, and that would be even more so if he asked her to test it out with him. "—I'd chase you out, wouldn't I?"

He thought she would get angry.

He thought she would say, "*So Nephren's fine, but I'm not?*"

"Hmm."

While Chtholly seemed upset, she didn't pursue the question and let go of the grip she had on Willem's ear.

"You behave now. You know it'll be big trouble if the little ones start copying her."

"Y-yeah?"

She gave his back a light smack and trotted off down the hallway.

What was that all about?

Willem cocked his head, not quite understanding the situation.

He was used to dealing with kids, not women. Thanks to the combination of the two, he never knew—not now, not back when—how to treat adolescent girls.

But there was one thing he had a hunch about.

"…She's pushing herself over something, isn't she?"

He wasn't very confident about that, though.

That was the impression he got from her when she acted like things were normal.

✝

Today was another day for the faerie warehouse managerial meeting in Nygglatho's room.

Fresh scones rested on a plate. Three kinds of jam sat out, ready for spreading. The kettle sat over the fire, a healthy bubbling sound coming from inside.

"...How's Collon's cold doing?"

"I don't think we're in the clear just yet. Her fever has started to go down, but it's still high. I'll be going into town tomorrow to get some medicine."

"Okay... If she starts having bad dreams and trouble sleeping at night, put this under her pillow," Willem said and placed a small piece of metal on the table, just the perfect size to fit in someone's palm.

It didn't seem decorative at all—just a metal lump.

"What's this?"

"An old talisman that prevents nightmares that result from illness. On its own, it's not restricted to any particular race, and it doesn't need activated venenum to work. Just put it under a pillow, and it'll do its thing."

"...Did you always have something this useful?"

"I never had it. It's warehouse equipment."

Nygglatho furrowed her brows. "Wait a moment. I should know about this if it's warehouse equipment. And I highly doubt a talisman so valuable, one that anyone can use *and* has function unrelated to battle, could make it through the budget."

"You knew it was here; you just didn't know what its function was." He tapped the piece of metal. "It's one of the pieces that sits in the middle of the blade to make up Seniorious."

"What?"

"I told you before, right? The Carillon are collections of wishes, a group of twenty-three or more talismans, tied together by veins of enchantment. That's why they're called *carillon*. So basically, if you undo the ties and pull them apart, one sword would become at least twenty-three different talismans. And Seniorious, by the way, is forty-one pieces."

"Seni...orious?"

"The other forty talismans are weirdly unusable, so I just left them in storage. Like, when are you gonna use a talisman for *'Blades unequipped with magic won't cut deep'* or *'Makes a sound if the holder calls themselves by anything other than their real name'?*"

"Put it back right now!!"

She slammed her hands on the table.

The teacups rattled precariously, but by some miracle, none of them spilled.

"Do you even understand what those Carillon—the dug weapons *are*?! They are the ultimate weapons that have *literally* kept Regule Aire afloat! And Seniorious is the most precious and important of these weapons!!"

"Yeah, I know." He nodded.

He was even confident that *he* was the one who knew Seniorious best in this world right now, in both a good and bad way.

"Then you should know better! You can't just tear the sword apart and use it as this—this little charm with a cute little trick! There's an order of priority to things, you know?!"

"Ha-ha. I was wondering what you were gonna say." He snorted. "A good night's sleep for Collon tonight is much more important than the fate of the world, right?"

"The entire meaning of the warehouse's existence will crumble from its roots if you say that again!" She clung to her head and squirmed.

"Well, that was eighty percent a joke, obviously. I'm at least trying to have good timing here. There aren't any enemy attacks coming soon, and it's not like Seniorious's compatible user can wield a Carillon in her current state. It won't be finding its way into battle for a while, yeah?"

"That's not quite what the problem is, but…" Defeated, Nygglatho heaved a deep sigh. "Very well, then. My superiors won't get angry with us if they don't find out, and I do want to help Collon in some way as well… Be sure to put it back in its spot when you're finished, okay?"

"Sure thing. I really like how understanding you are."

"Don't say that to me. Right now, I'm waist-deep in self-hatred."

She shook her head a few times, then downed her tea in one gulp. That seemed to somehow help fix her mood.

"—By the way, do you still have that talisman of yours? That, ah, language comprehension one you used just after being brought back from stone?"

"Yeah." He tapped his chest. "Haven't used it since learning the official language, though. It uses language as a mediator and just conveys intention as is, so all the subtleties of a conversation go out the window."

"I just had a thought. Why not sell it and pay back your debt all at once?"

"You know this is booty Glick and friends salvaged from the surface. I've been borrowing it all this time for free. I've gotta give it back at some point."

"It was yours on the surface in the first place, though, wasn't it?"

"If you put it like that, then we could even say that a number of the talismans here should be mine. Because even though I couldn't use higher-class swords, I've tried a good number of consumer-level Carillon... Oh, and by the way, what happened to Tiat's sword?"

"We're still in the process of testing several candidate swords. Right now, Ignareo has become a leading contender."

"That's kind of a low-class sword, huh. That's a good thing."

"It seems so. I am not exactly sure how I should feel, since I can't be happy about this in my position."

Only Braves could use the Carillon.

Braves were those who required strength: people who inherited lost techniques, people who were burdened with tragedy at birth, people who dedicated their whole hearts and souls with vows. Only those who had backgrounds that prompted others to say, *"They look like they could be very powerful,"* could actually gain that power in reality.

Being unable to wield a greater Carillon meant their necessity for that strength was not too powerful. It meant that one didn't have to give up their life for nonsense like fate or tragedy or vows.

"Tiat herself said she wanted a sword as strong as Seniorious, you know. She said she wanted to be strong enough one day to work in Miss Chtholly's place."

"I completely and totally understand how she feels, but I don't think that's possible."

With a wry smile, he reached out to the cup of tea she'd prepared for him.

He took a sip. It was more bitter than the tea he'd gotten used to drinking in this room. He really didn't know very much about tea, but maybe she used different leaves this time.

"It's not easy to gain her recognition. That's why I'm here now."

During a lull in their conversation, Willem's earlier conversation with Chtholly suddenly crossed his mind, and he told Nygglatho about it.

Just as he finished, she suddenly burst out into laughter, grasping her stomach as she did.

"That wasn't supposed to be funny, y'know."

"I—I knooow. That's why it's funnyyy!" Her voice shook, clearly a sign her abdominal muscles were still spasming. "You *do* understand what's going on, but you truly are the awkward one, aren't you?!"

"I don't get it."

"She was happy you would treat her the same way as me." Nygglatho let him in on the secret as she wiped the corners of her eyes.

"...So why would she be happy to be treated the same way as a troll?"

"I am her number one rival in love, the one she's most cautious of. To her, treating us both the same way means, at the very least, that you see her as a woman, right?"

"Oh, okay."

He took one of the scones, put a dollop of apricot jam on top, then threw it into his mouth. It was pretty sweet, but since the bitterness of the tea still lingered on the tip of his tongue, it didn't taste too heavy. He was a little impressed with how attentive to detail she was.

"...Rival in love?"

"That was a bit of a delayed reaction, wasn't it?"

"I wasn't expecting that at all. It took me a while to process it. Is it, what, that you and I could end up glued together in Chtholly's eyes?"

"Hmm, well, it sounds like it needs a little more supplementary information than that, but exactly."

"Okay, that makes sense," he said, munching on his scone. "I guess you are the only adult woman here, and I guess her way of thinking isn't too unnatural for a girl her age, huh?"

"Hmm, you're not entirely wrong, but there's one thing I hope you don't mind correcting?"

"What thing?"

"You don't need to say *her age*. Because I do have the same opinion as her, you know."

He didn't quite grasp what she meant right away, so he thought for a bit.

He unconsciously drank some more tea as he thought.

"I think rather highly of you as a man in general."

He choked.

The bitter tea slipped deep into his windpipe. He couldn't breathe. He struggled.

Nygglatho rested her chin on her folded hands, gleefully watching Willem as he writhed in pain.

"I'm rather serious when I think about being with someone like you. You're promising, mean to trolls but kind on the inside, we've already proven that we respect each other's work, you like children, we have similar tastes in food, we're both featureless, you're not bad looking, you could probably subdue my father without a scratch if he starts acting up once he's gotten drunk, and most importantly, you look delicious. See? You're a real catch."

"Wait. Some of the stuff in the second half sounded weird."

"So you accept that the first half wasn't so bad?"

That wasn't it.

That wasn't supposed to be the case, but he couldn't express it well.

"More importantly, they say that all the various races related to fiends branched off from the emnetwiht. Tribally, we aren't so far apart. So I may be able to provide a family for you that is related to you by blood. That should be the most definite reason for you to continue living in this world now. I would be so chuffed if I could provide happiness for you five, ten years down the line. That is the biggest reason why I wouldn't mind so much being tied with you."

He didn't really know how to react to what Nygglatho said.

The only thing he understood was that she was serious. Her mischievous smile and teasing quips were nothing more than her own way to hide her embarrassment.

"Well, my hopes to make sure Chtholly is happy are more important, so I won't be too aggressive in shooting her down. Yet she can't just ignore me due to the way she feels. Does that make sense?"

"Can I just ask you an awful question?" Willem groaned as he asked, stewing in his self-loathing.

"What is it?"

"Can I pretend I never heard any of this?"

"You truly are awful. But do whatever you want." She chuckled.

It didn't seem like her feelings were hurt. But Willem still couldn't bring himself to look at her.

3. The Large and Youthful Lizard

There were two kinds of people in the world:

Those who could have a cup of tea and calm down, and those who couldn't.

Island No. 68, the town center, the usual café.

The semifer waiter was so terrified of them that Willem almost took pity. He felt bad for thinking about how he just wanted the guy to grin and bear it.

"There's no tea at this shop, so I always wonder what I should have to drink..." Nygglatho tilted her head, eyeing the menu plate out of the corner of her eye.

"I ssshall have a medicssinal drink," the massive lizardfolk—Limeskin—announced with solemnity, his gigantic body balanced precariously on the tiny chair.

"Uh... I guess I'll have coffee."

"I was thinking the same... May I order some food as well?"

Without waiting for the other two at the table to answer, Nygglatho beckoned the waiter. She gave him their order, then unnecessarily added with a great portion of playfulness, "I'll eat you if our order doesn't come quickly enough."

"Seriously? You shouldn't threaten people so unreasonably like that."

"I wasn't threatening him. It was just a cute joke with a bit of bite."

She puffed out her cheeks.

"Okay, well, there's a bookstore on the corner there. Today should be the day when you go buy yourself a dictionary for Regule Aire's official language."

"Gosh, again with the teasing?"

"I'm just being considerate."

Willem rested his elbow on the table and his cheek on his hand and narrowed his eyes at Nygglatho.

Limeskin opened his mouth, and the quiet rattling sound of his laugh spilled forth.

"You two are quite clossse, aren't you?"

"Not at all."

One first needed to be aware of a lack of common sense in order to learn about common sense. In order to correct the mistakes of this mistaken troll, who thought she was acting with common sense, the person beside her had to explain to her in detail what was right and what was wrong. And Willem just so happened to be the only person around who could do that. So that was what he was doing. That was all.

"...And so? Why are we meeting like this today? There has to be a reason why you brought this big lizard, who was enjoying his privacy, all the way out here, right?"

"Oh? You can ssee thiss iss not within our current military affairsss?"

"Anyone can tell just by looking at you."

Now that he thought about it, he sort of felt like he'd come across Limeskin a good number of times: the rickety tower on Island No. 28, the harbor on Island No. 68, and the Winged Guard headquarters in Collina di Luce on Island No. 11.

In every single encounter, he was wearing his (probably custom-made) military uniform. The combination of his large stature and uniform gave an imposing, overpowering feeling, and it truly left a strong, lasting impression.

And yet, his outfit now...

"What kind of fashion sense is *that*?"

"It isss my daughter'ss choice. I am quite pleasssed with it."

".........Okay."

It was a bit...rough around the edges.

He wore a linen shirt and a leather jacket. It was the kind of style that young orcs were really into, with a number of garish threads embroidered on the shoulder. His whole look brought about an exquisite sense of unease, like it matched yet didn't quite match the milky-white scales that covered the man's body.

"Ssshe iss a beautiful girl, with sssssmooth sssscaless, like her mother."

"I'm not listening."

Willem hadn't known Limeskin even had a daughter in the first place.

Oh, he knew what he was up to. He was going to start bragging about his daughter to Willem, huh? Then that meant he had to be prepared for some counter-bragging. While they weren't related by blood and he had no intention whatsoever of comparing looks, no one could beat the combined power of his kids' adorableness and preciousness!

But if he spoke his mind, he might find himself caught in quicksand, so he clamped his mouth shut and kept himself in check.

"Willem. It's written all over your face that you want to brag about your own daughters in return."

That was Nygglatho. He at least wanted her to appreciate how he didn't *actually* say it out loud.

"Asss commander of our earlier lossss, I have been ordered a ssusspensss-sion. I sssshall not be wearing the Guard'ss uniform for a while now."

"That's a pretty lousy punishment, too."

The "earlier loss," the battle that led to the fall of Island No. 15, wasn't supposed to be the kind of battle where responsibility landed on the shoulders of the frontline commander anyway. But assuming it was his responsibility, then a suspension was much too easy of a punishment.

So in essence, this suspension was just for appearances, though Willem wasn't sure if it was meant for the satisfaction of the people inside or outside the Winged Guard. It was probably just a measure to forcibly put a finishing touch to the end of the incident that was the island's fall, since there were too many trade secrets at play that prevented proper disclosure of information to the public.

Organizations were a kind of organism. Once its body became large enough, it required some extra labor and irrationalities to keep on living. It seemed all those bothersome parts of organizations hadn't changed since the past.

"I do not need pity. A warrior'ss body ssometimesss requiresss a ressst. I am quite enjoying myssself."

Oh yeah. A (probably) grown man was just getting excited over his rare chance to dress up.

"Um, ahem." Nygglatho cleared her throat deliberately. "Should we perhaps get to the topic at hand soon?"

Oh, he'd brought up the subject himself, but he'd completely forgotten.

"First: I want to brainstorm with the two of you how we should be handling Chtholly from now on. Her current condition is unlike any of the previous faeries."

"Hmm."

Then came the food they ordered, the plates and silverware clattering on the tray. There was the pungent medicinal drink, two cups of coffee, and a plate with a thick-cut bacon sandwich.

"…Since mature faerie soldiers are weapons, there is no retirement or honorable discharge within the system of handling them. Though she is no longer a faerie, she is still, on paper, being treated like a faerie soldier. I want the management in the Alliance and the Guard to call an exception, so that we may let her step down from the front line."

"Ssshe isss no longer a faerie—isss thiss indeed true?"

That was the right question to ask. Someone tossing away the race they were born with and switching to something else was an absurd idea—and not easily believed. Willem still felt the same way. However—

"I checked many times. But the conclusion was still the same."

If the very person who would be the first to doubt those conclusions told him so, then he couldn't cling to logic much longer.

"Why not change the system itself? It's obviously not compatible with the current situation, yeah?"

"The very process for changing it would take time. Years, at worst. If she received orders to go on a mission in the meanwhile, just once, then there would no longer be any point."

"...To *sssome* extent, I am able to control which warriorsss are dessig-nated for missssionss."

"I know. That's why I invited you here today, so I may ask you directly to do something '*to some extent.*'"

"Asss a member of the Guard, I cannot resspond to ssuch a corrupt proposssal."

He took a sip of the medicinal drink. His elderly-looking appearance clashed with his youthful attire.

Now that he thought about it, how old was this lizardfolk anyway? A characteristic of their race, which had the greatest variance of stature among individuals, was that the age of maturity varied greatly depending on individual differences. Those of large stature spent a very long time growing up. He could imagine that this individual, who had a daughter and was in the high position of first officer, had to have lived for quite a long time to accomplish both of these things.

"But now, I am a private cssitizen on holiday. I have earnessstly conssssi-dered your requessst."

"Thank you, truly."

Nygglatho gave a very grown-up small sigh of relief.

For better or for worse, the act looked like it suited her real age.

There was a bit of a different air about her from when she was dealing with the little kids at the faerie warehouse. She was like a sister much older than him, like a mother close in age. This, too, was just another one of the many faces she wore.

"...Hey. There's something I just thought of, listening to you guys."

He didn't like how adults did things. He didn't do very well with that.

But it was probably the same for the other two. So he probably shouldn't be worrying too much about what he was or wasn't good with right now.

"There's a Great Sage, yeah? How connected is he to the Guard?"

Limeskin's shoulders shuddered slightly.

"That man isss the greatessst point of conssult for the Winged Guard. He hasss very few officssial authoritiesss, but hisss voice and influencsse hold great power."

"Perfect. So go ahead and announce this to the Guard so that this great point of consult hears you: The second enchantments officer has chosen Chtholly Nota Seniorious as the perfect sample for experimentation that might shed light on the very mysterious ecology of leprechauns."

"Wha—?" Nygglatho blinked. "What are you talking about? Experiment?"

"The enchantments officer is a research position, right? Then requesting equipment and material for research should be an obvious right. Even though it's just a title, I should be able to make this request. And if it goes through, then we can treat Chtholly independently of the other faeries, at least for the time being."

"That's only if it goes through, you know. And by Great Sage, you mean the Great Sage from the Regule Aire creation myth, right? Why are we talking about him, of all people?"

"We're old friends. We're used to asking for weird stuff from each other."

Nygglatho looked at him as though she was gazing down on a pitiful being. Looked like she didn't believe him. Oh well, it really wasn't important enough to make her believe him.

"Now what sssort of experiment would thiss be, exactly?"

"An observation on the process of recovery from a character breakdown and how natural stressors in an environment different from a battlefield might affect that. Tell 'im we'll be prescribing her special medicine as we watch her condition, too."

"...And so?"

"We'll take her away from battle and just let her live a regular daily life. And while we're at it, we'll also ask for a special budget for food for the faerie warehouse sometimes."

"And will the path presssent itsssself if the Great Sssage hearsss of thisss plan?"

"Yeah."

During their conversation on Island No. 2, Willem saw how greatly he and the Great Sage differed in perception. The Sage was the protector of Regule Aire and looked at everything from a long-term point of view. So he was detached emotionally when he looked at the faeries and could view them as pure military power. That was the kind of person he had to be; if not, then Regule Aire would have fallen long ago. That aside, Willem had a hard time accepting his way of thought and didn't want to be like him at all.

If he were to pass judgment from the Sage's point of view, he could not treat the single faerie Chtholly any differently, even if she was indeed the compatible user of the powerful Seniorious. He needed a system to preserve and maintain the required level of firepower for the long-term in order to keep the world safe. Those at the top should not be futilely pouring resources into Chtholly, one girl who may never be able to return to the battlefield.

"Whatever he says, he's still an honest guy. Even if he doesn't want to do it, he'll always look for the best way to deal with the situation in front of him. So the best way to get him to do something is to add value to another option. So if I make the request to look after Chtholly via the Guard, then he'll probably say yes. I don't think he'll pass up on an opportunity to get me to owe him."

"...What? Wait, don't tell me you're *actually* old friends?"

"Well, the real problem is how Chtholly's been a little off and what our fighting power will be like once she's gotten through all this. It'd be a huge burden to just have Ithea and Nephren attacking alone." He hesitated slightly before continuing. "And it's still early, but Tiat will need to mature, too."

"Well, about that, actually." Nygglatho raised her hand briefly, her expression darkening. "I received contact from Orlandry this morning. The surface research team was attacked by a large-scale Beast, and the airship *Saxifraga* was shot down."

"Huh?"

"Mm..." Limeskin's expression clouded over...or at least, that's what it felt like it did. "Did the warriorsss fight well?"

"The attack happened in the evening, just before takeoff. The pushback was a success. The good news is that *the two* were unhurt, though a bit exhausted. That being said, they have no choice but to stay on land overnight, and they have no way to get home, so the situation is quite grave."

"I sssee. Then ssssurely you ssshall sssend them the wingss of ressscue?"

"Most likely. But it is not that easy to arrange for an airship big enough to land on the surface. It might take a little time."

"Like piercssing a dragon'sss sssscaless with a needle, hmm? I hope it all goess sssmoothly."

Willem didn't know why they started talking about this all of a sudden.

He was pretty sure they were talking about all the battle-ready faeries still left in the warehouse. So why'd they change the subject to a "surface research team"—probably literally a group of people sent out by the Alliance to research the surface—that didn't have anything to do with that? He didn't get it.

"Uh, hold on a second, guys. I need an explanation."

The troll and the lizardfolk both turned to look at him.

"An explanation for what?"

"Why'd you wait until now to start talking about the surface? Even if finding another Carillon is the happiest news of the day, it's not gonna change the faeries' burden."

"What do you mean *why*?"

She looked at him blankly, then gazed at the ceiling in thought.

"Ah-ha!"

Suddenly, she gave a short burst of laughter.

It wasn't entirely unusual for Nygglatho to act eccentrically, and Willem was used to it. But he still wished she had a bit more tact about it.

"Oh, right, that's right. It's only been a month since you've come, hasn't it?" She chuckled delightedly. "I was so used to your desperate and awkward dad act that it doesn't feel like that anymore."

"Shaddup. *Desperate* and *awkward* are too much."

"So you're aware you act like a dad, then?"

"Just tell me. Who on earth have you been talking about?"

"Um, well… Right now, how many mature faerie soldiers do you think there are in the warehouse?"

"Three, not counting Chtholly. And if not counting Tiat, since she hasn't been assigned a sword yet, then two."

"Sorry, but the correct answer is five. Ithea, Nopht, Nephren, Rhantolk, and finally Tiat."

Willem looked up to the ceiling.

"There are two names I haven't heard before. Where'd you hide them?"

"Can't you tell where I'm going with this? It's there, over there."

Nygglatho pointed downward.

There was nothing on the table. There wouldn't be anything on the floor. What Nygglatho was gesturing to was much, much farther away.

Willem snagged a piece of the bacon sandwich that sat before Nygglatho, tossed it into his mouth, chewed and swallowed it, then let the first word he thought of roll right out of his mouth without a filter.

"Seriously?"

Seriously.

The troll and the lizardfolk nodded in unison.

4. Gray Days atop the Gray

Now, this is the story of what happened on the surface.

The general turn of events went just as Nygglatho described. The surface observation airship *Saxifraga* was attacked by a Beast and was shot down.

It appeared from a fierce sandstorm.

Its silhouette didn't look entirely unhumanoid. It had a torso with a head and arms and legs growing out of it. But getting any closer would completely knock that image off the table. A reddish-brown shell covered its mansion-size body, and peeking out from the gaps in the shell were thousands of eyeballs.

It was Beast Number Four, the One who Twists and Swallows—Legitimitate.

The same could be said for all the Beasts identified as yet, but their behavioral principles remained unknown.

In both the stricter and wider senses of the word, all living things naturally existed to survive. In the stricter sense, it was for the individual's survival. In the wider sense, it was to keep one's species alive in the world for as long as possible. Eating and sleeping and looking for a mate—everything could be logically concluded as either type of survival. Every form of life was born, lived, and died with these goals ingrained in their very being. That was the way it should be.

But it was apparently different for them.

How they handled reproduction was unknown, but at the very least it was evident that each individual was not particularly thinking about how to survive. Though they didn't easily die, they acted in a way that put their lives on the line as they went after the beings of Regule Aire.

From the era five hundred years ago to now, they had only one goal—

Kill the living. Or maybe it was even to break the moving. There was probably no distinction between the two in their minds.

Of all the Beasts found on the surface, Legitimitate was one of the most commonly encountered. At the same time, however, it posed a rather low threat.

It relied on sound and movement to search for its prey.

First things first when encountering one was to shut your mouth and cease all movement. Then, if you moved so slowly that it didn't take notice, you might be able to escape alive. That was the basis for its categorization as a "low" threat, and it was information that was considered common sense among salvagers, and that was an order that should have been thoroughly explained to the research team during the mission briefing.

But panic erupted almost immediately anyway.

As the researchers tried to escape the scene to preserve their own lives, the Beast chased them one after the other, a single swipe of its arm cutting them all cleanly at the waist. The final cries for help and pools of blood brought about another wave of panic, and the damages spread rapidly.

The worst part came afterward.

At the time, the research team's supervisor, the first mechanics officer, was inside the *Saxifraga* as it rested on the sand. When he saw the tragedy unfolding outside his window, he immediately cried out and rushed to the control room. He unsheathed his ceremonial sword and threatened the operators, making them turn on the furnaces to begin takeoff.

It relied on sound and movement to search for its prey.

The Beast immediately heard the deep humming sound of the driving furnaces.

Its large body, close to a small mountain in sheer size, dashed along the sand with frightening speed and rammed its raised arms against its prey. There was a dreadful crushing sound. The simple but ironclad ship was sliced through as though it may as well have been thin linen, and all its ballast spilled out. With all its ballast gone, the ship tipped over, its body twisted, and began to tear apart.

Then—

"What the hell are you doing—?!"

The two leprechauns finally arrived on the scene and cut the Beast down, and the commotion immediately came to an end.

There were eighteen dead, almost half of the whole crew. All the horses brought for transport and other animals had perished as well.

And the airship *Saxifraga*, collapsed on the sand, was now no longer capable of flight.

†

The sun set.

Everyone was tired.

To make matters worse, the airship was already nothing more than a giant husk.

Without any other choice, half of the survivors crawled into tents, settling down to sleep in an attempt to rid themselves of consciousness. The rest each built their own fire and sat around it.

"—I'd say you girls did pretty well." The boggard man spoke vacantly as he spun his stick of skewered meat.

The fire made a quiet cracking sound as it slowly roasted the horse meat.

"Usually this'd end up in total destruction, but the fact that we've got this many survivors is a miracle. We should be counting those people, not the dead."

"You really think you can call this survival?" Nopht responded, wrapped in a blanket and staring at the flames. "The ship can't fly, which means we can't get back to Regule Aire, you know."

"There's a high-speed ship out there that's got our status report. We just need to take it easy for a bit, and help will come before we know it."

"Take it easy, huh?" The girl bit into the meat. "We can't escape to the sky once night comes, and we'll have to spend every single hour of the day on this sand. One or two of 'em should be fine, but if we get too many Visitors, I don't think we can do much with just the two of us."

"Eh, that probably won't happen. We probably won't see another Four, at least not for a while," Glick said plainly as he began to roast a new skewer.

"Why's that?"

"Legitimitate's behavior is such that it won't live near other Fours. I guess you could also think of it the other way around—you won't find another Four after it's appeared once."

"First I've heard of that." Nopht's eyes widened.

"It's a pretty well-known story among us salvagers. The other Beasts don't run around actively, so as long as we stay put here, we should be able to keep the threats to a minimum. Even if we're not optimistic about it."

"Huh." Impressed, Nopht turned to the other girl beside her. "Did ya know about this, Rhan?"

No answer.

Of course, the indigo-haired girl was wrapped in a blanket, staring silently at the wavering flames, not even moving a muscle.

"...What, she tired?"

"Nah, she's not. This is what happens when she starts thinking. She enters her own world and can't hear voices or any other stuff around her at all."

She took a skewer in hand, made sure the meat was cooked all the way through, then shoved a piece into Rhantolk's mouth.

"Mgh?!"

That brought the girl back.

"Mrh mrgh!"

Rhantolk's eyes widened in bewilderment, and a moment later her cheeks turned bright red.

Hot, hot, hot, hot. Still wordlessly, she flailed her arms and legs about under her blanket, but even then, she didn't spit out the food in her mouth.

"Don't get too carried away in your thoughts when you're eating. Show respect to the food by concentrating on what's in front of you— Hasn't Nygglatho scolded you like that plenty of times already?" Nopht said, mimicking a lecturing tone as she pierced new pieces of meat onto the skewer. "This girl, I swear. You'da spaced out until your meat turned to coal if I left you alone. This is our first helping of real food in a long time. You need to savor and enjoy the meat, otherwise it'd be rude to the horses!"

"B-but still, you don't have to suddenly shove it in my mouth!"

"Okay, okay, but eat your veggies before you complain. Sheesh, they're burned to a crisp."

"I—I know! Gosh!"

Her face red, Rhantolk reached out to a skewer by the fire.

"I wouldn't take the skewers over here if I were you. Boggard seasoning won't suit your tastes at all, ladies."

"I know!"

"But now that you mention it, I do want to give it a shot."

"Bad manners, Nopht!"

Glick chuckled with a low voice.

"...Ah, is something wrong, Glick?"

"Nah, nothing. I was just thinking about how you act more like teenagers than I thought. I heard an acquaintance of mine called you guys the ultimate weapons that were protecting Regule Aire. I thought you'd be more military-like or that you would be sulky because you'd given up on life. You're kinda cute, somehow."

"Huh. First time we've been called cute." Nopht smiled, amused.

"I still plan on properly sulking, though," Rhantolk added, blowing on her skewered vegetables.

Rhantolk thought as she munched on her burnt carrots.

The Beasts were full of mysteries.

In fact, they were nothing *but* mysteries.

Five hundred years ago, everyone gave up on learning about them. And in those five hundred years since, no one had risen up to try and learn about them again.

They were the ultimate calamity, unleashed upon the world by the cursed race, the emnetwiht. They were described in a way that was easy to understand yet explained nothing, and she hadn't thought any more about them. But.

She remembered.

—*The emnetwiht race should never have been started. This was the first and greatest sin of the Visitors, who created them.*

That was a passage from the ancient text they had recently excavated, a phrase Rhantolk had just deciphered.

The people freed the Beasts, and the world filled with the gray truth—

That was probably a mistranslation.

After all, it wasn't as though she'd studied the emnetwiht language. She just knew basic grammar and a few words here and there. She was trying to force her way through a difficult passage at her skill level, so of course she would make a mistake somewhere.

It had to be so, otherwise there were too many oddities.

The Beasts were supposed to have been created and freed upon the world by the emnetwiht.

But if she read it and interpreted it as it was in the text, then the Beasts were *not* created by an emnetwiht hand but instead—

"You can't just start thinking again *right after* I told you not to—you'll mess up your digestion!"

"Mgh?!"

This time, a nicely roasted potato was stuck into Rhantolk's mouth. Hot, hot, hot, hot.

5. Island No. 49

How was one supposed to go down from the top of the sky?

Even an infant knew the easiest option, and that was to go to the nearest island rim, face outward, and take a step forward. After flying for literally over a thousand marmer, one may give the motherland a passionate, *hard*-core kiss. Passage that came at the simple cost of one life. Cheap stuff.

But if someone fancied a different way of going about it, then it became exponentially more difficult.

Adding the condition of being able to come back made it even more so.

They said Regule Aire was contained by a large barrier. If a regular airship that was typically used for going among islands tried to pass through this barrier, all of its gauges would lose control, and it would no longer be able to fly properly. To prevent that, all machines needed Wessex Bordering, a protective measure specifically for flying to the surface. But the work required to furnish that also took quite a bit of time and money, so it couldn't be done at the snap of a finger.

It would take six days, even after pushing the timeline to its limit, to install the Bordering on the *Plantaginesta*, the semi-great whale-class transport airship that would retrieve the survivors of the research team and the results of their study from the surface.

That was the explanation he got at the Winged Guard base on Island No. 49.

"Why d'ya need such a big ship, though?"

"Choose your words carefully, Second Officer. I am the first officer, you know? I'm more important than you."

A gremian wearing a guard uniform screeched in displeasure.

The gremian only came up to Willem's waist, and it was too easy to overlook his shoulders. And on his shoulders was a proud collection of badges with intricate designs on them.

Oh, right, military organizations are pretty strict with the hierarchy. The absent thought went through Willem's mind a little too after-the-fact. He once fought alongside the armies of the Empire and the old kingdom five hundred years ago. But he had a feeling he didn't actually belong to either of them. It was pretty new to him.

"My apologies, First Officer. This is a voyage into a new frontier for me, so please forgive me."

"H-hmph. Very well—that's good enough." Though he appeared taken aback by the sudden change in demeanor, it seemed to have calmed his mood. "Now, you were asking why we needed such a large ship, yes? Very well. I shall explain it to you, since I am a very kind first officer. Because I *am* a very kind first officer, after all."

Ugh, make him stop.

Willem hid his true feelings behind a smile and bowed his head. "I give you my thanks, very kind First Officer."

"Very well." The gremian, now in a much better mood, began to babble. "To put it simply, we have lots of cargo. This study originally stemmed from the discovery of an emnetwiht ruin whose original form was comparatively more well preserved. This was a long-term study for the very reason that we estimated there would be plenty of results to be taken home, and in reality, we received a report that they discovered an incredible number of relics that absolutely could not be left behind on the surface."

"…The dangers to the research team grow greater every day we delay the rescue."

The gremian looked at him like he was nuts.

"Everyone on the research team is aware of the risks involved in gaining the surface's wisdom. And as you may already know, they have two of our Winged Guard anti-Beast protective *weapons* with them. It's for times like these we let those guys at the Alliance look big, so they've got to play their part, you know."

"……"

The air froze.

A bird fell from the sky outside the window.

A cat napping in the shade of a tree gave a yelp and ran off.

The soldiers working hard at their jobs in the same building as them all suddenly felt a dreadful, agonizing chill for no reason. Some fell from their chairs, some gave out cries, and some immediately went on guard.

"Mm, the muscles in your face seem to be tense. Is something the matter?"

The gremian looked at him blankly, not appearing to notice the odd events happening around them.

"Oh, it's nothing. It is perhaps just as you say, wise First Officer."

"Okay. It's hard to read you featureless's expressions. Oh, by the way, I've got just the reading material for you. You may be a second officer just for decoration, but you'll probably understand how important this study is when you see this."

He tossed a file in Willem's direction.

It was a simple document; ten-odd report-looking pages were tied together with string. The title, scribbled across the front with messy handwriting, read, *Ground Level K96—MAL Ruins Second Study Report.*

I don't care about what they're picking out from the ground after all this time, Willem thought, but the file did pique his interest. He knew they were putting a good amount of money and people into these land studies. What was it the Alliance and the Guard were looking for with all that effort?

"May I look inside?"

"You can't take it out of this room, though."

Willem took the file in his hand and opened it.

The first few pages had data on their coordinates and ship routes. He didn't understand any of this technical stuff, so he skipped it.

Next was a map of the entire ruins, sketched in relief as accompaniment for the excavation.

Apparently, five hundred years ago, that used to be the location of a town with about three thousand emnetwiht residents. The main road was paved with large cobblestones and was lined with cheaply built group housing. There was a large structure to the northeast that might have been something like a city hall. Presumably, there was a forest surrounding the town at the time, and there was a total of four rivers of all sizes both within the town and outside it, two of which seemed to have been redrawn as man-made canals.

"……"

Damn, most of this is pretty close, he thought absently to himself.

There were indeed about three thousand people living in that town, and the roads were paved with cheap-looking cobble, and there was once a pretty large forest surrounding it. The number of rivers was a little off, though; if they were also counting man-made canals, then they were missing two rivers.

The form of the town shown on the map looked exactly like a town that was once in Imperial territory called Gomag—Willem's hometown.

He looked for a facility on the map just outside of town. It was a shabby wooden building that was already pretty worn down five hundred years ago. He couldn't find it. Maybe their study hadn't reached that far yet, or maybe there was simply no trace of it left.

"That's not the interesting part, is it? Go to the next page, the next page."

The first officer urged him on, so he turned the page.

There was a simple list of discovered artifacts and talismans, pictures and documents.

It felt like the center of his brain had turned to lead. His vision swam over the letters that comprised the list, but what was written on the page didn't reach his brain.

"That document was created by the report sent in from the messenger ship that arrived just the other day. So that means all the prizes written there are still waiting to be collected on the surface now."

But how much does that really matter? Willem thought.

If you want a picture painted by an emnetwiht, I'll draw you all the pictures you want. So just hand over that pen and paper. You want pottery? I'll make you some pots. You want some books? I'll write you the greatest timeless masterpiece there ever was.

Then—

"Dug weapon…Lapidemsibilus…?"

His eyes were drawn to a phrase near the middle of the list.

"Yes, there was apparently an inscription on the hilt. It seems to be quite a high-ranking weapon. With this, Regule Aire's protection has grown a level sturdier!"

He shouldn't listen to how delighted the first officer sounded.

Lapidemsibilus, the blade of stalwart defense of life.

It was the Carillon that one of Willem's old companions, Navrutri, used. But why did they find it *there*, of all places?

He should have been off to battle with the Visitors, just like the rest of them were. The Tihuana District, which was acting like a battlefield at the time, and the town of Gomag were so far away, on practically opposite sides of the country.

No, that aside, more importantly…

"I see… Lapidem, huh! That's one way to do it!"

The world before him suddenly shone brighter.

"Urm, hmm?"

He grabbed the gremian's arm and nodded his head up and down excitedly.

"This is a fantastic military achievement, courageous First Officer! The research team has certainly accomplished a great triumph! All of Regule Aire must welcome the heroes and their accomplishments!"

"Y-yes, of course. I am pleased to see you understand all this." Overwhelmed, the gremian nodded several times. "And, you see, I'm also thinking that we may have to add further protection to the *Plantaginesta*, which we're sending to go get them. So I want a dug weapon with a compatible spirit to go along."

He pondered.

It sounded like an obvious request.

At the present, there was no forecast for any future attacks by Timere. The forecasts were reliable, and the larger the scale of the attack, the earlier it could be predicted—in short, there wouldn't be any large-scale battles in the few days to come, at least. So the risk was low in the faerie soldiers leaving Regule Aire at the moment. Of course the Alliance would ask for the faerie's protection, and of course the Winged Guard would accept their request; it was hard to say that it was very reasonable for this decorative second officer to raise a fuss about it here.

Based on all that, he thought some more.

"...May I make a request, oh generous First Officer?"

"Hmm?" The gremian tilted his head.

"Do ya think you can add another seat to that ship?"

He took his leave from the room, walked down the halls to exit the base, and rushed along the tranquil and rural roads to get to Island No. 49's second city.

The closer an island's number was to No. 1, the closer to the center of Regule Aire it floated. And in almost the same manner, that applied to how accessible it was and how many people lived there. The larger cities were mostly concentrated on islands numbered forty and below, and islands numbered seventy and above were mostly untouched, left in their natural state.

Island No. 49. It wasn't a pretty number.

And here, just like the number it represented, was a city that sat somewhere in the middle—not very big but not small enough.

"Oh, there you are!"

She sat under a dark-green umbrella in an open-air café that faced the plaza.

Before her was an empty glass of juice and a partially eaten cream cake.

Chtholly was sitting there clearly bored when she saw him cutting across the plaza to approach her, and she gave him a big wave.

"Sheesh, you're so late! I was getting tired of waiting!"

"Sorry 'bout that. Lots of stuff happened. Ready to go?"

"Wait, let me eat this first."

Before she even finished speaking, she made the cake sitting on the plate vanish in an instant.

It was a technique that made Willem, who was, by the way, a seasoned veteran, watch in bewilderment.

"Mmm."

And indeed, Chtholly's mouth slacked sloppily.

Chtholly never ate sweets at the dining hall in the faerie warehouse. Her reasoning being that she never wanted to show her unbecoming expression to the little ones. That made sense now. He felt the explanation was pretty persuasive.

"Sorry about that. Now, let's go shopping."

She stood, took the hat that occupied the seat next to her, and placed it on her head.

This neighborhood wasn't particularly discriminatory toward featureless. There really wasn't much point in going out of the way to hide her head. He'd explained that to her before they left the warehouse, but she insisted, *"It's fine. It doesn't really matter, does it?"*

"What order should we do things?" she asked. "I think we should visit the bookstore last. Everyone made so many requests for me to pick up, so there would be a lot to carry. I don't think it'd be so nice to lug such a heavy load around."

"...You look pretty pumped about it, though."

"Really? You must be imagining things." She started to walk off before she even finished speaking. "It's not often we get to walk around outside, just the two of us. I probably look excited because of that. By *not often*— Actually, I think this is our first time doing this, right?"

"Of course not." Willem sighed. "The first time we met, we ran around all over the place. Don't tell me you forgot about that, too?"

"Oh... Right. Ah-ha-ha!" Her expression was guilty, and she tried to brush it off with a smile. "Well, come now, let's not mind the little things. We'll have to stop and go home before the sun sets if we don't hurry."

"Was that a little thing?"

She glared at him with a terrifying expression.

It was a regular town.

Trade didn't particularly thrive here. Very few tourists came to sightsee. The population was neither too big nor too small. It wasn't an especially safe or dangerous place. It had no specific stand-out characteristics, a place that could only be described with the adjective *regular*. That kind of town.

And so the town was made with nothing but the pursuit of the residents' comfort in mind. The small roads were paved with brick. Small staircases were buried between the gaps of buildings. Boggard children ran about in delight, waving their short sticks.

Willem ended up carrying way more bags than he'd prepared himself for.

They found a nice-looking park, so they decided to take a break.

"Hey."

They sat together on a bench, leaning on the backrest.

"Hmm?"

"You really okay with this? You know you're allowed to do what you want outside of the island now, right? You don't have to just follow me and go shopping; you can do literally whatever—"

"Okay, enough, no acting like you need me to spell everything out for you even when you know why!" She poked him hard. "It doesn't matter if it's on the island or outside. I just wanted to stay together with you."

Oh, right. He thought she would say something like that.

"I mean, there are some places I want to visit, some things I want to see. But that doesn't quite mesh well with the place that I want to be, so there's not much I can do about it. Right?"

Ugh. He couldn't take this anymore.

This pure girl, who grew up knowing nothing about male creatures, just happened to meet *a* man in a somewhat dramatic fashion. The feelings a girl would have in a situation like this were strong, simple, and terribly cruel.

"What on earth is it that's so good about me?"

"Not telling."

She smiled impishly.

There was a short, comfortable moment of silence.

A small thought bubbled inside him, a feeling of wanting to stay this way forever.

"They told me they were gonna put a faerie soldier on the ship to the surface," he murmured quietly.

"Mm."

"It would still be too much for Tiat, so we took her out of the options. We stressed over which of the other two we should send, but we decided on Nephren."

"Mm."

"And while I was at it, I negotiated directly with the guy and made him put in space for me."

"…Mm?"

Chtholly's head spun around to look at him.

"Why, though?"

"Unlike the thing at Island No. 15, it doesn't sound like they're putting up some kind of barrier that you can't enter or leave or whatever. You can go if you want to. The first reason why is because I'm not gonna stay waiting for someone to come home again." He folded his fingers as he counted his reasons. "There was the name of a sword I just couldn't ignore on the list of treasures they found on land. If it's the real thing, then I want to get it as soon as possible. That's the second reason."

"A sword?"

He ignored her question and gazed up at the sky.

"You've been pushing yourself pretty hard recently."

"…What are you talking about?"

"Don't play dumb now. I can sort of tell by the way you've been acting recently. You've lost some of your memories, haven't you? Or are you still in the middle of losing them now?"

A waffle cart stopped on the road beside the park and opened for business. The sweet aroma wafted and filled the air around it. A child walking along the road began to beg for change from their parents beside them. The parents dealt with it coolly at first, but their attitudes changed slowly as the sweet scent tickled their noses. *"It's just before dinner. You shouldn't make a habit of spending all your money on sweets. Oh well, I suppose it can be a treat just for today. Excuse me, can we have a hazelnut cream and berry medley waffle, please?"*

"How can you tell?"

"I just told you; I can sort of tell by watching you."

There was something off about Chtholly's behavior. It weighed on his mind, so he watched her. That was how he first took notice of some things. Some things he would never have noticed had he not watched her.

"I see. You were worried about me."

"You thought I wasn't?"

"No, of course not."

She looked happy but troubled.

"—Let me just say this now, but don't get too excited about what I'm about to tell you. It's really not much more than something that *might* be possible." He gave his disclaimer. "But it's the sword they found on the surface, the one I told you about. Its talent manifests as one that keeps its user's body and mind in the best condition possible. At least, five hundred years ago, I saw with my own eyes as it canceled out attacks that make you act unhinged emotionally and destroy your memory. If we had that, it might solve your memory problem thing."

She blinked.

"You...speak so calmly of reckless acts, don't you?"

"The trick to making recklessness into a reality is to put it into words."

"I'm not sure if that's something you should be proud of." She chuckled.

They could hear the guy at the waffle stand yelling loud and clear, *"Thanks a bunch!"*

"Okay, I won't get too excited about it, then. But I can trust that you won't give up on me, right?"

"Yeah, sure."

"How long will it take, then?"

"I dunno. Probably ten days, or maybe a little longer than that."

Chtholly stopped in her tracks.

"...I'm going, too," she murmured.

"Huh?"

"I just said, I'm going, too. I'm not gonna stay waiting for someone to come home again, either."

"What?"

"It's fine. I still remember who Nopht and Rhan are. I wasn't too close with them, but I don't think they'd say anything weird if I saw them."

"No, no, wait. They definitely won't allow that. It's not like they can add more seats to the airship's capacity, and it's not like they'd wanna take along someone without any skills as a touri—"

He watched as Chtholly's expression turned demonic.

He realized he'd made a slip of the tongue.

Willem recoiled slightly, overwhelmed.

"Are you going to finish that sentence with the word *tourist*?"

"—Nope. That's not what I meant. You know, it's dangerous on the surface, and it's not really a place you can just waltz onto, and, uh..."

He realized that he was now ready to put his foot in his mouth.

"Oh? Does it look like I'm going to be waltzing anywhere?"

Chtholly spoke slowly, her calm voice cutting deep.

"No, wait, you know. Let's cool off a bit and chat about it."

"I am furious. I am *definitely* going, too!"

"Wait, wait, but they aren't gonna let you go anyway!"

If he had to give a conclusion, it was that they would let her go after all.

After they went back the way they had come and talked to the first officer, he easily gave her permission to come along. He added Chtholly's name at the bottom of the passenger list and handed her a simple form of identification.

"—Don't tell me you're mad at me?" Chtholly asked hesitantly on the way back home. "You look really grumpy."

"Of course I do." He gave a deep sigh. "You know why you got permission so easily, right?"

"Because…the second officer introduced me?"

"That's just a prerequisite. That's not enough to let a regular civilian without any proof of skill or without a background check go along on such an important mission."

Most of the islands of Regule Aire didn't have anything like a census registration system. That was because in places like these, where many different races and individual values mingled together, there was a limit to how the residents could be managed by documents. According to the law on most islands, citizenship was purchased from the city in the form of tax. Although it was convenient for leading a daily life, it wasn't compulsory. For instance, like Willem's neighborhood on Island No. 28, there were some areas where most of the residents didn't have citizenship—and consequently, it was a dangerous place.

And so Chtholly, even after just losing her status as a faerie soldier, could still at least be considered a "civilian." What came after that was the problem.

"Usually, to tag along on military missions, you need skill that won't hold the others back and the trust that you won't do anything unnecessary. So there's no such thing as being too cautious when it comes to taking along civilians."

"But I did get permission, didn't I?"

"Basically, that means there've been other officers in the past who've taken civilians along as secretaries. And they've all probably been the opposite sex of the same species."

"...Um?"

He recalled the first officer's nasty smile when he brought back Chtholly.

"It *means* they brought their lovers along, justifying them as secretaries."

"Lovers..." Chtholly slowly repeated the word, as though it was in a foreign language she was hearing for the first time.

"And it means he thought we were the same as those guys."

"...Oh... I see now." Chtholly thought briefly. "I think that's all right."

"No, it's not."

"Then will you at least make me your wife?"

"No, come on."

There came a distant chorus of Carillon bells.

Willem stopped in his tracks, a sense of nostalgia overcoming him as he listened to the end of the chorus.

The sun was setting. Evening was drawing near.

"Well, I guess it's not too bad. It's not like we still need to keep up appearances, and I don't want to be apart from you, either."

"Oh, it makes me so happy to hear that, but that's not a proposal, is it?"

"Of course not."

He looked at her with exasperation, as though wondering why she was asking that *now*.

Chtholly smiled wryly in agreement.

"Let's go, then."

He looked away and walked off with a long stride.

After a moment, Chtholly started rushing after him.

"Hey, wait, wait! Slow down!"

"Whoops, I totally forgot, but we might miss the ship to Island No. 53."

"...What?!"

Island No. 68 was on the outer periphery of Regule Aire. There were no public commuter airships that went straight there, and in order to find a ferryman to get there, one had to first go to an island somewhat nearby.

So Willem had a fair reason to pick up the pace like he did. It was not a way to hide his embarrassment at all.

"We won't make it home today at this rate. C'mon, hurry up."

"Wait, hold on—these bags are so heavy!"

The two strolled casually and merrily through the townscape as it was slowly painted crimson.

†

What am I? the girl thought.

Ever so slowly, her memory was chipping away, her personality breaking to pieces. In the end, even now as she was cracking, would she still be called *Chtholly*?

She could now remember only about half of her fellow faeries' names at the warehouse.

Even if she took the time to study and re-remember them, her memories of them would never come back.

Whether it be when she was in her own room, or in the dining hall surrounded by her sisters, or helping Nygglatho, something felt off about the daily structure she should have established by now.

Bubbling up from somewhere unknown was the baseless feeling that this was not where she belonged.

She thought her own situation was painful.

It was bitter, sad, and lonely.

And she wanted to hold all these feelings dear to her. Because when those were gone, that would probably be when the girl who was once Chtholly Nota Seniorious would completely disappear.

✝

Chtholly told all the faeries in the warehouse that she would be taking the airship to the surface.

"Miss Chtholly, are you leaving us again?" the green-haired girl asked in cheerless surprise.

"Hmph." The pink-haired girl looked away weakly. It seemed her cold still hadn't gone away.

"It's not something to brood over. It's not like she's going away for an eternity," the purple-haired girl said lightly.

"Um... Please be careful. Please, please do be careful," the peach-haired girl begged, tears brimming in her eyes.

"We'll have a welcome home party ready for you when you come back," Nygglatho added with a smile—a slightly strained, forced smile.

"Personally, I want to tell you not to do it." Ithea looked like a mother who'd relented to her own child's selfishness.

"I'm sorry. But I really don't want to wait."

"Oh well. There's a bitter love monster stuffed inside your skull that's crammed full of romantic feelings, I know. Pulling it away from its crush would only make it wither and crumble away, I know."

Chtholly frowned.

She wasn't *that* far gone, she wanted to protest.

But she knew it didn't sound very convincing, so she decided not to. It was an adult's wise judgment not to do anything unnecessary. Probably.

"I'd want to go with you if possible, but I guess I can't. It's not like I could do anything to help you if I came along anyway."

"It won't really be anything you have to worry about. I'll be sure to find you a souvenir from the surface," she said and gave a thumbs-up.

Ithea didn't respond.

She decided to leave Seniorious behind.

She wouldn't be able to use it even if they brought it along anyway.

And…someone who was working hard for their own happiness was not qualified to touch that misery-obsessed thing, regardless of words like *faerie* or *compatible wielder*.

"Good-bye, partner."

She stuck her tongue out at it.

And those were her parting words.

6. Reunion

She knocked on the door, but there was no answer.

She turned the doorknob, and it wasn't locked.

"Hello…?"

She pushed the door open. It was dark and empty.

Oh, right— Tiat finally recalled.

The owner of this room wasn't in the faerie warehouse at the moment. She had boarded an airship headed for the surface to retrieve a couple of the other older faeries who were out on a long-term mission. It would still be a few days until she was back.

"Um… I came to return the book I borrowed…"

She hesitantly stepped into the empty room.

She managed to muffle her own footsteps as she cut across the tidy chamber.

She placed the book she held to her chest neatly on the desk.

And then, she noticed something sitting on the corner of it.

There was a large, stylish dark-blue hat and something else, something that glinted silver.

"This is…"

She recognized it. It was a silverwork brooch with a clear blue stone embedded in it.

It looked really good on her senior faerie, and Tiat was often envious of that. She still remembered what the elder faerie had said to her.

"Thanks. But I know one day soon, it'll probably look really good on you, too.

"When you get just a little bit older, I'll give it to you."

She'd found herself flustered at the time, because that wasn't why she felt envious. She hadn't wanted the brooch itself; she just wanted to express how well such a grown-up accessory looked on her. But she was a little happy that she said that to her, just a little.

…Maybe she forgot it?

She could feel a bit of mischief bubbling inside her. She'd grown up a bit since then, hadn't she? Maybe now she was enough of a woman for it to look good on her.

She was just going to try it out.

She gulped. Slowly, she reached for the brooch.

Her fingertips brushed the silverwork.

"…No, I can't."

She pulled back.

Even if it was just to try, she felt like if she touched it, she would end up losing something incredibly precious.

Incidentally, the *Plantaginesta* was originally a large-scale transport ship. The philosophy behind its design was different from that of commuter airships, and it was built exactly so that it could carry more materials with greater reliability. To put it simply, not a single part of the ship was designed with a comfortable ride in mind.

The entire vessel pitched and rolled. Strange pipes stuck out here and there in all the rooms and corridors, the smell of oil clung to the air, obscene graffiti had been scrawled on the walls, empty cans of meat paste lay scattered across the floor, and so on and so forth.

Willem wouldn't have thought anything of it if the environment was just plain old bad. But just by adding that sway unique to airships, it easily pushed the limits of his discomfort.

Their estimated flight time was forty-two hours.

It was a hellish forty-two hours.

Ground level, K96—MAL Ruins.

The location of the felled surface observation ship *Saxifraga*.

"The whole world's spinning..."

With shaky steps, Willem stepped down onto the gray sand.

The sole of his shoe sank about the thickness of his palm into the soft sand. The absent thought of just how bad this footing was crossed his mind. Merely walking on it would quickly drain his energy, and now there was the added danger of falling over if he ran or fought.

He lifted his gaze slightly.

Before him was a gray ruin. There was a row of strange-looking monuments, as though someone had poured a muddled gray dye over crumbling stone buildings.

This was once a small town.

It was at the edge of Empire territory, quite a ways away from the Imperial Capital.

It hadn't been particularly big or prosperous. It was not on any of the major trade routes, and it didn't have any particular specialties it was famous for. It was a town that just quietly built its own history over centuries, one that was supposed to keep on building.

He leaned over and grabbed a fistful of sand.

The gray dust smoothly slipped from the gaps between his fingers.

"It hasn't really hit me like I thought it would."

Not a single emotion he'd steeled himself for made itself known.

He couldn't force himself to feel sadness or frustration now.

It wasn't like he didn't feel it was real. Willem was oddly accepting of the fact that this was the fate of what was once the town of Gomag, his home.

"…Are you okay?"

"Yeah, nothing to worry about."

Nephren had appeared at his side at some point, and he answered her question and stood.

"It doesn't look like there's nothing to worry about. You're very pale."

"Probably just from motion sickness. I'm really not bothered by this at all."

"You're really not bothered after coming here?" A blustery wind swayed the sleeves on Nephren's protective sandstorm cloak. "That worries me more. Isn't this your home?"

"I'm fine, really. My birthplace is gone. My home now"—he pointed upward—"is in the sky. Right?"

Nephren reached up with both arms. She grabbed on to Willem's head and pulled his face closer to her own.

She made him look deep into her eyes.

"…You're not acting?"

"Of course not. Now lemme go; it'd be a pain if someone sees us."

"But I didn't do anything embarrassing."

"It's not what you think but what other people watching think."

"Reeee—"

There came the scratching sound of running footsteps on sand.

"—eeeeen!"

It came from his blind spot.

Accompanying the yell was a kick that flew straight at him, and it struck him right in his side.

Thinking it would be the same as when Collon and Pannibal attacked him, he stayed in his spot and took the kick. That was a mistake. It was a much sharper and heavier attack than he imagined, and it threw his body off to the side. It was super painful.

The boy…oh, no, girl who attacked him grabbed Nephren's shoulders and shook her hard.

Still lying on the sand, Willem raised just his head and watched them.

"Hey, you okay? What'd that perv do to you?! He didn't get what he wanted, did he?!"

She had spiky vermilion hair, and her eyes were just a shade darker. Though he'd never seen this girl before, it matched the appearance he'd heard about beforehand.

Nopht Keh Desperatio, designated compatible with dug weapon Desperatio.

"No, Nopht." Nephren seemed to be in slight pain as she wriggled. "He's not a pervert who does stuff to children; he is someone who is a problem *because* he does nothing."

"Man, I had no idea you'd be the one coming to rescue us! Awww, you're still soooo li'l!"

She wasn't listening.

Squeeze. With the world's biggest grin on her face, Nopht wrapped Nephren in a hug from head-on.

"...It hasn't been more than a month since you left the warehouse. I'm not going to grow that much in that short a time."

"Really? It feels like I haven't see you in forever—" Suddenly, Nopht stopped. "...Hey, you went to that fight, too, didn't you, Ren?"

"Hmm?"

"The one when the big Six attacked."

"Oh..." Nephren nodded, still in Nopht's arms. "We went and fought."

"Then tell me, how valiant was Chtholly?"

An odd expression crossed over Nephren's face.

"Um, very valiant, I suppose."

"Ah." A sad smile spread across Nopht's lips. "I don't really know how to put it," she began, "but I dunno. She wasn't very nice, and I didn't think we'd get along very well, and that still hasn't changed. But after coming here, we got into a situation where we didn't know if we'd get home alive. I regret it, just a little. I don't care if we just hated each other. I don't care if all we would've done was argue, but I wish we'd talked more."

Willem slowly sat up.

He could now see two new girls drawing nearer from the airship.

One was a face he knew well, and the other was one he didn't know at all—but that, too, matched the description he heard earlier. It seemed there was no doubt that this was one of the two faeries sent to the surface.

Rhantolk Ytri Historia, designated compatible with dug weapon Historia.

Now he knew they were both safe, Willem felt his worries ease.

"The Beast on Island No. 15 must've been strong. Yeah, it's not normal that we could only win if Chtholly opened the gates. And you're all in one piece, so she musta done it. She opened the gates, didn't she?"

"Ah..."

Nephren very obviously didn't know what to say. He'd never seen her like this before.

"She probably said it was to protect everyone, didn't she? She's so straightforward and really pretends like it's no big, but I'm pretty sure she was super scared but talked like it was nothing, and I know—"

The binds on her heart must have come loose since this was the first time in a long while she was seeing her fellow faeries from the warehouse. The more she talked, the more nonsensical her words became. She herself would probably soon wonder what on earth she was talking about.

The indigo-haired faerie, Rhantolk, tapped her on the shoulder.

"Nopht."

"What? I'm busy right now." Nopht sniffled lightly, stopping her ramble.

"Take a deep breath."

"Huh?"

"Breathe in, breathe out. Then when you calm down, turn around."

She was an obedient kid at her core. Nopht did as she was told and took a deep breath, exhaled, then turned around to look behind her with a confused expression—

And she froze.

"...Um..."

A red-and-blue gradation waved with changes in the wind.

There was Chtholly, standing there with a guilty expression on her face.

"I guess, um... Long time no see?"

Chtholly for some reason spoke with a rising inflection, and though she was facing Nopht, her gaze was pointed in the wrong direction.

"Muh…"

"Muh?"

"Monsteeer!!"

Nopht released Nephren and sprang off into a run at an astonishing speed, one where the unstable footing on the sand was absolutely no problem.

"H-hold on, wait a second!!"

Chtholly followed after her. Chtholly was rather fast on her own. Even though she wasn't fast enough to catch up, she kept the distance equal, not letting her get too far ahead.

The two lively girls ran through the husk of the ruined city on the destroyed earth.

"Who do you think will win?"

"Hmm… I bet my dessert that Nopht will fall and Chtholly will catch up."

"Then I bet the same on Chtholly getting tired out first… It's been a while, Rhantolk. I'm glad you're safe."

"And I can say exactly the same back to you… I am truly glad you're both all right. Truly."

Rhantolk squeezed her palm around Nephren's tiny hand.

As he listened to the conversation beside him, Willem murmured, "They sure are happy…," and watched carefully as the two ran into the distance.

This Present Radiance
-my happiness-

1. The Suspicious Emnetwiht

Nopht was giggling, ticklish throughout the entire procedure.

"Eh-he-he-he-he-he-he-he-he-he-he."

Her arms and legs flailed about every which way, and it was a hassle keeping her still.

Chtholly started to help partway through, and it would have taken even longer without her assistance. There was no doubt it wouldn't have ended with just one bruise around his eye.

On the other hand, Rhantolk was trouble in a different way.

Whenever Willem put a finger to her back and applied pressure, the girl exhaled with an oddly alluring noise. She had an adult air about her that didn't really match her age to begin with. Whenever he heard the voice, he felt like he was doing something he wasn't supposed to, and he lost his touch. It almost took twice as long to finish the treatment than he had originally estimated.

During treatment, Chtholly's pointed gaze into the back of his head hurt his heart considerably.

When he asked, the faeries explained there were sporadic attacks from Beasts even after the *Saxifraga* fell. Though none of them was a major threat and all were easily disposed of, Willem knew there was a possibility, so he checked to find out that, just as he thought, both of them had minor venenum poisoning.

Venenum conflicted with a person's life force in the first place. Activating venenum was essentially causing one's own life force to malfunction on purpose. And activating too much of it at once, or keeping it activated for long periods of time, or reactivating it over and over in a short period of time, could make the crippled condition easier to keep coming back again and again, and that made it even harder to fix.

He had just now applied one of the ways of dealing with that on the two girls. First he stimulated the applicable points on the body, adjusted the blood flow, then forcibly relaxed the rigid muscles. In the old world, it was known as a practical battlefield medical technique.

"Phew. How's that? Feeling better?" Willem asked, tired after all that, and the two girls glanced at each other.

"Uh… My body feels real light. It kinda feels wrong."

"I don't think it's easy to relax if we're not still exhausted after a fierce battle."

The treatment itself produced the proper effect, but regardless, he was met with somewhat spiteful responses.

The two girls had been acting like this ever since Willem introduced himself the day before.

He somewhat understood how they felt.

To them, the man who was Second Officer Willem Kmetsch was an unknown character who suddenly appeared before them and started acting like he owned them. Even though his identity was confirmed and both Chtholly and Nephren vouched for him, he hadn't done anything to show he was trustworthy, nor had he taken any time to build up their trust. It was natural they would be cautious around him, and he understood that to an extent.

He understood, but…he felt like that wasn't the whole story.

"But you're an emnetwiht, right?"

When he asked them directly, Rhantolk readily gave him the reason why they were cautious around him.

"It would be sweet if you were just a role player, but Chtholly and Nephren vouched for the truth. That means you are *the* deadly race that broke the world. I don't know if I can accept you so easily."

That made sense. Of course that was it. Even though none of the people he had revealed his own race to acted in that way, it was a second, careful thought that told him he had just been lucky. Her line of thinking was rather typical.

"But it's not like I did anything on my own..."

"Now that you said that, if someone said you were suspicious, then that carefree posture, that lax attitude, would make you look even more suspicious. It's like you're trying to hide what you're really thinking. You're like a man who's used to deceiving women... Though I know there's no end to it once I start questioning you."

If you know, then stop questioning me.

The world should be viewed through a simpler lens.

But wait, what did she mean by *"used to deceiving women"*? That was a terrible misunderstanding. He wanted her to take that back.

"I give you my thanks for saving Chtholly from her planned death. And judging by the quality of the skill you used to heal us, I know that your abilities themselves are worth praise. It must be true that you were a...Quasi Brave in the old world, a battle-capable individual. You, on your own, are much more specialized for battle than we are, who are born and die to fight. But that is not enough data to determine whether or not you are dangerous."

If she was willing to recognize his skills to that extent, then all he needed was just one more step.

"Do you know how the emnetwiht spread the Seventeen Beasts throughout the world?"

He'd heard a bit from the Great Sage. An anti-Imperial organization at the time, called True World, developed the Beasts; they were a kind of biological weapon.

"A biological weapon?"

Yeah. That's what he'd heard.

"Then there must have been a living creature that acted as an elemental base for it. Does that sound familiar?"

No. He didn't think it was that important. He thought they'd probably captured some new kind of monstrous being.

"I see."
"I see"? *Really? That's it?*
"Yes."
...*I see.*

"I don't really hate people like you."
Nopht's answer was an easy one.
"You don't act high and mighty at all. You look kind of poor, actually. If Ithea and Nephren trust you, then you're probably not thinking about doing bad stuff. You actually look like you're not thinking about anything."
He wasn't sure if he should be happy or sad about that.
"But, nah, not for me. I trust Rhan's eyes the most. Sorry, but if she says she can't trust you, then neither can I."
So that's where it was going in the end.

"You shouldn't worry too much about it."
He must have looked pretty bummed about it because Nephren approached him.
"Those two are always like that. They're not usually the type to truly hate people, so I'm sure they'll be nicer to you before long."
"Yeah... I guess so."
They didn't seem like bad people. Rhantolk was just going through things in her own logical manner, and Nopht just trusted her and her process.
He didn't feel like he should hate them.
"Thanks," he said with gratitude, and Nephren tilted her head. "You're always on my side, aren't you? It's a big help."
"Hmm... That's not really the reason why," she responded with her usual hard-to-read expression. "You just look like you might break if I leave you alone."
"...Do I really look that helpless?" he asked, a slightly hurt tone to his voice, but Nephren stayed silent and did not respond.

†

It sounded like the reloading of artifacts was going smoothly. One crate after another was stuffed into the lowest part of the airship—the hold, which was filled with the pungent scent of metal and oil.

Willem received permission from the operations manager and popped open one of the crates. He pulled out the inside article, wrapped tightly in a dirtied, tattered rag.

"You better be careful there. If ya don't watch out, you might find yourself with an emnetwiht curse!" an orc worker warned him with a charismatic smile.

"Thanks for the consideration, but no worries here. I'm an emnetwiht."

"Ha-ha! Mate, stuff like that doesn't embarrass you at your age?" With a laugh, the worker left.

"...He probably thought I was having teenage delusions."

Whatever the truth was, the emnetwiht was a legendary race, the embodiment of evil. Anyone would normally think it an embarrassing fantasy if he suddenly announced himself to be one. He would have to be more careful in the future.

He turned his attention back to the thing in the cloth, the large sword made up of tens of different pieces of metal, and lifted it to his eye level. There was no doubt about it—this was the pure-grade Carillon Lapidemsibilus.

He didn't know why they had excavated it here, of all places. Navrutri was from West Garmando, and he didn't think very well of the Empire. Willem couldn't think of a reason why Navrutri would come all the way to this remote part of the Empire after his fight with the Visitors and Poteau.

"Eh, whatever."

Navrutri probably had some good reason. Willem wouldn't think too hard on it. Right now, the question of how the sword itself was faring was much more important.

He glanced over the veins of enchantment to see how they were doing.

They were spectacularly tattered. It was practically unusable in this state, and he was unsure if he could repair it to its original state with his skills. He would have to take it apart and examine each piece carefully.

"—Why are you here? What are you doing?" Nopht poked her head out from behind a crate. "If you wanna steal that stuff and sell it for profit, it has to pass through the Alliance anyway, so there's no point, y'know."

"Huh, I'm kind of offended you'd treat me like some scoundrel." He wagged his finger. "I'm a terrible, evil emnetwiht. If I'm gonna be plotting stuff, it'd be on an even bigger scale."

"For real?"

"For real." He cackled.

Nopht seemed genuinely intrigued.

"So…like what? Like crashing this airship or something like that?"

"Nah, I'd die, too."

"But carrying out evil deeds without any care for your own safety does sound kind of cool."

"You're too sentimental. True evil doesn't need stale pride and stuff like that. Always be easy on yourself—and kind to nature while you're at it. That's the most important thing if you're gonna call yourself evil."

"For real?"

"For real."

He cackled.

"Oh yeah, I remember now. I'm going to be adjusting this one, so I may as well do you guys', too. Can I borrow 'em?"

After this and that, Willem borrowed the girls' swords.

Then he found an empty storage room.

Steel, copper, and tin sheets had been thrown together like a mosaic to create a makeshift wall. On it was hastily written, improper graffiti. There were small cracks here and there in the underbelly of the pipes that ran across the ceiling. There was only one clasp left on the grate over the air vent, and it seemed like just one good shake would make it fall. There were a number of tools, probably brought in when they were working on the Wessex Bordering, sitting by the wall.

An indescribable, foul odor assaulted his senses the moment he stepped into the room.

It wasn't a very comfortable place. But at least here he wouldn't have to worry about the wind and the sand, and more importantly, it was quiet.

"I'm not really in the position to ask for a nice room anyway."

He untied the string that kept the two swords on his back and placed them by the wall.

He picked one of the two back up, sat on the floor, and slowly began to loosen the venenum that ran throughout the blade.

"—Initialize adjustment."

About half of the thirty-eight metallic fragments drifted through the air one at a time, finding their own spots and stopping in place.

Unlike the other time when he fixed Seniorious, this room wasn't very spacious. It would be difficult to take this sword apart completely to adjust it. He figured he would do a proper adjustment after they got back to the faerie warehouse, and for now he would just go with a simple inspection and repair. Luckily, there was no one else here, and if he could immerse himself in his work, then it would be over fairly qui—

"Oh, there you are."

Chtholly poked her head out from the other side of the door.

She wore roughly hewn working clothes. Her hair was tied back so it wouldn't get in the way.

Ever since they'd boarded the airship, Chtholly had made herself known in different parts of the ship and continued diligently helping with little jobs here and there. She was, after all, assistant to the enchantments officer, who really didn't have any work. There were no tasks they had to attend to in the first place, so if she wanted to be of use to someone, then she had to find work herself.

"Sheesh, you can't just disappear on me like that. I'm your secretary! I have to at least know where my presiding officer is at all times."

"...Uh, well..." It was so sudden, his working hand stopped in surprise. "Your 'secretary' position is nothing but a title; you know you don't actually have to do any work, right?"

"It's not very convincing at all when you say it."

He had nothing to say in return.

Why did she want to work so badly?

"If I don't do anything, then you'd actually become someone who abused his power to bring his useless lover onto a battlefield. And you know, I don't like the sound of that."

"'S not something you need to worry about."

"But I do worry about it." She puffed out her cheeks like a child. "Hey, can I watch you?"

"I don't mind, but it smells bad in here."

"That's fine. There are plenty of other rooms that smell much worse on this airship."

Nothing seemed *fine* about it at all. The thought crossed his mind, but if that made her feel better, then he wouldn't bother raising a fuss. He casually waved her in and took in his audience.

"Is that Nopht's sword?"

"Yeah."

With the tip of his finger, he gently tapped one of the metallic fragments—a talisman. The piece slid through the air, and once it reached the place where it belonged, it froze.

There was a clear metallic sound, like a metallophone.

Chtholly lowered herself onto a nearby toolbox.

"It is beautiful, but it's not very romantic in here."

"Way better than a sandstorm, though. Just bear it for now."

"I guess so."

A question suddenly crossed Willem's mind. "You still remember the night I adjusted Seniorious?"

"Yes, I do." Chtholly nodded. "I'm taking care not to activate any venenum, so it doesn't really feel like my memories are chipping away right now. It might just be that I don't realize it, but at the moment, it doesn't feel like an inconvenience. I still remember Nephren, and Nopht, and Rhantolk, and…Ithea. I'm not very confident when it comes down to details, though."

"Uh…huh."

She hadn't mentioned Willem Kmetsch's name just now because she probably didn't need to reconfirm who he was. She probably hadn't forgotten him. Otherwise she wouldn't be here, talking like she was now.

The talismans quietly sang their terrible song.

They wordlessly spent a few moments like this.

"…Hmm?"

An odd feeling overcame him.

"What's wrong?"

"It's not broken."

"Of course not. If it was, then Nopht would be having a hard time right now."

"No, that's not what I mean. What I mean is…" How should he explain this? He spent a whole two seconds thinking. "One of the elements that shows a Carillon's abilities is something called its slayer level. It's a thing that establishes what kind of enemy the sword is especially effective against."

"O-okay."

Chtholly seemed briefly perplexed by the sudden onslaught of jargon, but she was going along with it anyway.

"As it keeps cutting down enemies of a certain type, it develops a peculiarity or a murderous specialty that starts sticking to the blade. You ever heard of the Dragonslayer? Titles like that are given to swords whose slayer levels have tipped far in one direction."

"O-okay…"

It probably didn't make much sense to her, since all they did was use their swords against the Beasts. It's not like she'd ever seen a dragon anyway.

He kept going.

"This sword is the Kinslayer."

"...The what?"

"Its specialty is killing kin. This sword exists only for emnetwiht to kill emnetwiht, and it's not really used for anything outside of that."

"Wait, that's weird. Nopht uses that sword to fight against the Beasts."

"Exactly, it's weird. That's why I thought that maybe its functions associated with its specialty were broken or something."

Upon checking, he found that the sword Desperatio was worn out as a whole and its functional efficiency was low, but the functions themselves were operating normally, almost to the point where it was hard to believe that its last maintenance was over five hundred years ago. The spinal root was healthy, and the veins of enchantment still had some strength in them.

"Well, today I'm just doing some emergency repairs. We can save mystery solving for another da—"

"Then there must have been a living creature that acted as an elemental base for it. Does that sound familiar?"

Chtholly looked at him in doubt again when he suddenly fell silent.

"...Now what?"

"Nothing." He shook his head.

An awful supposition sat square in the middle of his mind and wouldn't move.

He was thinking too much. He would convince himself he was.

Sure, if he thought of it *that* way, then it would solve many mysteries at once—the reason why the Seventeen Beasts destroyed the world with such frightening speed.

According to the history books, two entire countries disappeared from the map in just a few days.

By the beginning of the following week, five countries, four islands, and two oceans disappeared.

And by the beginning of the week after that, maps themselves had become pointless—

"......"

No. That couldn't be it.

Of course it couldn't. If *that* was the truth, then it was impossible that Great Sage Suowong hadn't realized it. And if he was aware of it, then why didn't he tell him...?

"If you wish to say something, then you must tell him everything. The man's attitude may change if you expose one or two secrets of the surface that you've kept hidden."

There was a reason why.

What kept him quiet, what kept him from saying anything was none other than Willem himself.

Willem had turned him down, saying that he didn't care about the things he'd already lost, that the only things he was focusing on were the things within his reach.

At the time, he didn't think his own attitude was appropriate. But he didn't regret it, even without using the word *appropriate* to quantify his behavior.

And what it was that he could hold in his arms now—

"Hey, what is going on?"

It was her third time asking.

Willem stood without a word and walked over to where Chtholly sat.

"Wah—"

And he pulled her into a tight hug.

"...Seriously, what is going on?"

Chtholly reached out to pat Willem a few times on the back, as though soothing him.

"Aren't you surprised?"

"I'm super surprised."

"Aren't you flustered?"

"I am flustered, actually. My heart is pounding. I don't know what happened, but I know it's unusual for you to show me weakness, especially since you're usually putting on a face. My feelings of happiness and how much I want you to feel better are both so much greater than my surprise or fluster."

"…You…"

"Right now, you look like you'll vanish if I leave you alone. It's really embarrassing, but I can't just ignore it."

He tightened his hold around her.

"H-hey, that's too much…"

"You're a good woman."

"…Sorry, I couldn't hear you very well. Could you say that again but louder this time?"

"It's nothing."

"Ugh, hey, you sore loser! Say it again! Just say it again for me!"

"Marry me."

"Nooo— Oh, wait, um, what?"

This time, Chtholly squirmed about, flustered in his arms.

There was no way he would let her get away, so he tightened his hold on her even more.

"Rather…he seems like stubbornness incarnate. He holds only one purpose within him. He sees no value in anything that has nothing to do with that goal. So he will not bend. He will not stop. He will persist."

He finally found it.

He was once a shadow of a Brave who failed in protecting what he should have kept safe, who never returned to the home he should have gone back to. But he met Chtholly, came to the faerie warehouse, and discovered a new way of life.

He finally had something he wanted to protect.

He finally found a home he could return to.

He finally felt like it was okay for him to keep living, that he was worth it and qualified to keep on living. And so—

*   *   *

"I wanted to make Chtholly happy."

—He was going to make Chtholly happy.

He clung to that wish.

He wanted to forget about the past. He wanted to keep on thinking of nothing but the present and the future.

"Ahhhh…"

He realized the girl in his arms had, at some point, stopped struggling, so he checked on her.

Maybe she couldn't breathe anymore, or maybe she'd passed the limits of her own shock, or maybe it was both—but either way, Chtholly sat there in a daze.

2. The Smiling Princess in the Icicle Coffin

That was probably a dream.

That was the first thing Chtholly thought when she woke up.

It wasn't entirely impossible. The punch line was a proposal, after all. Those weren't the kind of words that would come out of Willem, even if she shook him upside down. It wasn't very realistic.

But…when she asked Nopht and Rhantolk about what happened yesterday, they said, "That officer guy asked me to let him borrow my sword" and "He came back in such a good mood that it seemed creepy." Their answers made it seem like her dreams and reality were getting mixed up. What was up with that?

"What is it about the emnetwiht?"

When Rhantolk asked her, Chtholly responded extremely naturally, "I-i-i-it's nothing; don't worry about it." There was no way she was going to open discussion with, *"I think he proposed to me, but it might've been a dream."* Even if she did, all she would get was Rhantolk's cool gaze and a burst of laughter from Nopht.

Maybe the best choice in this situation was to ask the man himself.

"—*Hey, did you propose to me yesterday?*"

Nope, impossible. It was absolutely impossible. Especially since she was aware now that her memory was vanishing, it seemed kind of…tacky.

"What do you think it means to be happy?"

Instead, she took the question that came to her mind and tossed it Rhantolk's way.

"—That's a rather philosophical thing for you to ask. Are you starting a religion or something?"

"No, it's just a more personal thought of mine."

"I see." Rhantolk closed the book she was just about to read, and a pensive look crossed her face. "First of all, happiness is different for everyone. There are people who are happy from simply eating. There are people who are happy just reading books. There are people who place great importance on living to the fullest. There are people who only feel fulfilled when they accomplish something. There are people who are happy when others are happy, and there are those who are the opposite, when they're a nuisance to others."

"…Yeah, I suppose you're right."

There were many different kinds of people. There were many different kinds of hearts. There were many different kinds of desires. So that meant the number of forms happiness could take matched all those variables. Logically, that was a given.

"But most people aren't self-aware. They don't know what it is that is connected to their own happiness. Yet they all say they want to be happy. They don't even try to learn what exactly those words mean."

"Aha!" A smile spread across her face. "That strikes home. I certainly am guilty of that."

"People like that may be able to *realize* happiness, but that doesn't mean they can *become* happy. The most important thing is to not look away from your own heart. Does that answer your question?"

"Yes." Honestly, she hadn't expected such a detailed response, so she was taken slightly aback, but of course she couldn't say that. So she finished with an honest, "Thank you."

She went to the mess hall to have breakfast.

By Willem's request, faeries Rhantolk and Nopht were now allowed to use the mess hall. She invited Rhantolk to come along, but she refused, saying, "I'm not very comfortable in places with people I don't know." Dragging along someone shy wasn't going to get either of them anywhere. And so, Chtholly went alone.

Now then. She once again started thinking of what happiness was to her.

She slapped a sweet-boiled lemon peel onto her toast. She stuffed it in her mouth. A titillating sweetness and acidity spread throughout her mouth. She was happy. But this happiness probably wasn't it.

It was a faerie's state of being not to have any ambition-like ambitions or, rather, to not even think of having them. That was because faeries had no time. It would bring only sadness to dream of the future with a life that might not even still be around the next day. And that kind of situation still held true for her, even though she was no longer a faerie.

But Willem would never allow her to give up. He would tell her that even with a life that wasn't guaranteed the next day, she should hold her head high and head full speed for the day that came after. That was incredibly difficult and cruel, but she had started to like that part of him. She probably couldn't escape it anymore.

Thorny pills.
A gecko with
lovely round eyes.
Soaking wet
baked goods.

An incoherent string of images flashed in her mind. It seemed her encroachment was advancing steadily, albeit slowly. She should probably end up feeling pathetic in this kind of situation, which was reminding her she had no future, but she was used to it already, and she did not even waver.

She waved her hand to chase out the interruption in her mind and started thinking again.

She could think of only one thing. And that keyword was *marriage.*

Her old favorite book said it was synonymous with a woman's happiness. She didn't personally know any married women, so it didn't quite strike any chords with her, but for now, she would believe that it was and start her fantasy.

She remembered what Nygglatho said to her the other day. Marriage would make Willem family, or something, and keep him in the faerie warehouse forever.

She started daydreaming.

The setting was ten years from now. The stage was… Well, the faerie warehouse as it was now was fine. There was Willem, who was a little older… It was hard to imagine him like that, but giving him a beard and stuff was probably good enough. She placed herself, now more grown-up, right by his side. The two of them had children of an unknown race. Two boys and a girl. One of the boys looked like her, and the other two looked like Willem. The three were energetic and mischievous—they would run off and fall over and get all covered in mud the second she looked away, and she would chase them and catch them and throw them in the bath, then Willem would lazily remark, *"It's great they're so energetic,"* as he baked his cake—

(*…I can't remember very well, but I think that's exactly how it is right now.)*

She cut off her daydream.

Somehow, that wasn't it. That certainly was a very happy life, but if someone asked her if that made her much happier than she was now, she would find herself tilting her head in thought.

A redheaded child
clutching her stomach,
rolling about in laughter.

Her past life was so loud. Now was not the time for her to be paying attention to it, so she begged it to shut up.

"Why are you making such funny faces while eating toast?"

She suddenly noticed that, at some point, Nephren had come to sit next to her.

"You've been so weirdly bubbly this whole morning. But I mean, you're always weird."

Gulp. The toast caught in her throat. Milk—where was the milk?

"Did Willem say something to you?"

Hrgh. The milk entered her windpipe.

"...I knew it. I was right."

She coughed, choked, and swallowed it. She started to calm down a little.

"Wh-what made you think that?"

"It's obvious." Nephren's answer was simple, and Chtholly found herself speechless. "But that's why I'm worried," she continued, ripping her bread into smaller pieces.

"About what?"

"The both of you lately have this look in your eyes like cats that've lost their homes."

...Oh.

"It doesn't look like you want to talk about it, so I won't ask. But something's been happening since your hair started changing color, hasn't it?"

Well...

"Um... I guess."

"You can always talk to me if you want. I can't do much but stay by your side, but...at least I can do that much—" Nephren cut herself off, finishing with a sentence that didn't quite make sense.

"Okay... Thank you."

Ithea, Nephren... How did she come to be surrounded by such wonderful people? For a moment, she forgot about her situation and felt happiness.

†

That was probably a dream.

That was the first thing Willem thought when he woke up.

It wasn't entirely impossible. The punch line was a proposal, after all. Those weren't the kind of words that would come out of himself, even if he was dangled upside down. It wasn't very realistic.

"…No, it's definitely impossible."

He had to face reality. He had definitely embraced Chtholly and said some stupid stuff to her yesterday. He knew why he did it. It was because he never wanted to let her go. No, that wasn't it. It was because he wanted to stay with her forever. No, that wasn't it, either. It was because he was going to make her happy for the rest of their lives.

…He should stop. The more he thought about it, the more his thoughts rolled in absurd directions.

He took his thoughts a step back. Desperatio, the emnetwiht-killing sword. The monstrous beings that acted as ingredients for the weapons that were the Seventeen Beasts. If he put those two things together, the answer was simple. Whether or not she knew about Desperatio's specifications or not, that faerie Rhantolk had also arrived at the same conclusion. That was why she was so hostile to him, since he was an emnetwiht.

So in essence, the conjecture was that the Seventeen Beasts were emnetwiht themselves, modified in some manner.

He felt nothing.

He didn't want to think about it.

If that was the truth, then that would greatly change the meaning of "the emnetwiht destroyed the land." They didn't just create the cause of destruction. They were the cause of destruction itself, and even more so the very symbol of walking destruction.

"Nah, it can't be."

There was a big, gaping hole in that explanation. The Beasts' growth rate talked about in the tale was much too fast to be rationally possible.

This should go without saying, but in order to completely rearrange one living thing into a different creature, it would take a considerable amount of work and time on top of mythic skill and technique. Vampires were legendary monstrosities that had a soul-infecting talent, and even that required three days at the least for their victims to transform into vampires. He'd heard the Seventeen Beasts, on the other hand, completely wiped out a number of countries mere days after they appeared. They were incomparable.

"I'm definitely thinking too much," he concluded and nodded to himself.

Now he had one less thing to think about.

Now what was left was the result of him proposing to Chtholly.

"……"

Yup. He wouldn't be able to look her in the eye for a while.

"We made the research adviser mad," the first officer muttered, his shoulders drooping, the expression on his face like a child scolded for his mischief.

"Ah, I see." Willem gave a vague response, not really sure what the context was. "You brought along an adviser, of all things? Haven't seen 'im round."

"Well, it's a civilian salvager the Alliance hired and the research team brought along. He apparently has plenty of experience, so they wanted to take his opinions into the highest possible consideration."

"Huh. What happened?"

"Well, you've heard we won't be taking off for another five days, haven't you?"

"I guess."

For Willem, who was not interested in the adventure and allure of the surface at all, there was no reason for him to want to stay in this place for an extended period of time. He would want to immediately fly away if that were possible, but he knew things weren't that simple. They had to check on the health of the research team members, reload all the excavated articles into the ship's hold, and collect necessary tools and machinery from the *Saxifraga*, which would be left behind—there were many things they had to do, apparently.

"We also have to think about our budget, so we can't extend our stay any longer than that. But just bringing back the artifacts we've collected so far would put us in the red."

"Well, sure."

"And so tomorrow, we've decided to send out an additional, larger excavation team underground." The gremian first officer raised a purple finger, flaring his nostrils as though proud of his great idea. "The members will be mostly made up of Guard members, since we want the results to go to the Guard. We will have the Alliance take care of miscellaneous duties here on the surface. It's up to you if you want to come along. How about it?"

"No, thanks. I see, and that's what made the adviser guy mad?"

A veteran hired by the Alliance would certainly not be happy to hear that they were pettily trying to earn achievement points by carrying out such extravagant feats with a group made up entirely of Guard members.

"No, that's not it." With his raised finger, he scratched his bald, purple head. "He told us not to send so many people underground at once. That it's against general surface activity theory."

"…So why is that?"

"I don't know. I asked for his reasoning, but he didn't give any. It's more than likely a myth of sorts. Not everyone is logical and thinks about things like we do. Those sad people who believe in unreasonable conventions as absolutes because of their narrow world view will always be around, no matter the time and place."

"Ohhh. So is that what you told that adviser, imprudent First Officer?"

"It is." The truly imprudent first officer dropped his shoulders in disappointment. "I had no intentions of misstating things. But I did not hope to dismiss his experiences and beliefs, either. Do you think I could ask you to follow up on his feelings?"

"I don't mind," Willem said as he thought, *What a pain*.

"Things that one person will think are right will *always* be huge mistakes to a different someone with a differing background. If you ever feel like you've failed, remember that."

"…I understand."

The gremian nodded bitterly.

†

When Willem asked the workers walking down the corridor where he might find that adviser guy, they told him he was headed toward the research equipment vault in the hold. Equipment vault? That was near the bottom of the ship, a confusing place that was hard to walk around in. Why would he be there?

He really thought it a pain in his neck, but he wouldn't ignore it. He pulled open a heavy trapdoor, climbed down a rusted ladder, weaved through rooms filled with nondescript metal items scattered about, and headed for the lowest part of the ship.

They said the adviser was a civilian salvager hired by the Alliance. He tried to imagine what kind of person that would be, but all he could think of after hearing it was a "salvager with lots of experience" was Glick and company. They were, after all, a remarkable bunch who excavated one of the extinct emnetwiht—and even got him revived.

"Is the research adviser here?"

He came to the equipment vault. He pushed open the semi-airtight door and began searching for someone who might fit the description.

And there was Glick, clad in heavy gear meant for venturing on the surface.

"...What?"

"...Huh?"

The two men stood staring at each other, an indescribable air enveloping them.

"What we call our theories come from an accumulation of all our rules of thumb." Glick muttered his grievances, his bad mood apparent. "Like, we know how easily it can get mixed up with superstition. There are definitely some theories that I'm unsure of myself. Like, they say *flatten your ears if the sounds of water stop underground*, and I get it if you're, like, an ailuanthrope or something, but what should races like us do?"

Maybe they should just be happy they're at least not being told to "curl your tails."

"By 'rules of thumb,' do you mean big groups that go under never come back?"

"It's not always. There's a clear drop-off in survival rates when groups get to about seven people. That's why civilian salvagers don't really do work in big groups."

That made sense. He didn't manage to ask how many people that simple first officer was planning to send down, but he probably wouldn't cut people from the group.

"I see. Now I know why you're mad." Willem nodded. "Next question: What's this?"

"Dust-proof cloak, muffler, and goggles."

"Why're you giving them to me?"

"The sandstorm's pretty bad today. You're screwed if you go out without preparing."

"But why are we going out?"

"Today's the only day we can go underground."

How did that make sense?

"Since you're here anyway, there's a treasure I wanna show you. Can't bring it up to the surface, though, so we'll have to go down to where it is."

"Why are you making me do this?"

"Just come with. I never thought I'd come down here to the land to run into you, y'know. The Visitors're blessing us. We'll be punished if we don't take this opportunity."

How did *that* make sense?

"—Oh, hey, perfect timing. You wanna come along, missy?" Glick looked up and called out to someone behind Willem.

Thinking Nopht or someone had come by, Willem turned around to see none other than Chtholly's back as she was trying to slip away undetected.

Chtholly turned around slowly, her expression suggesting she didn't know what to do.

(…Ah, shit.)

Willem again recalled what happened last night, and his own expression became vague, his eyes darting around, unsure where to look.

But Glick remained blissfully unaware of the tension between them.

"You're a secretary, right? So Willem's support is part of your job. Three's the perfect number for going underground. We get less blind spots, and the other two can cover for any blunders the third makes. We could also leave someone on the surface for backup."

He cheerfully pulled out another set of dust-proof cloak, muffler, and goggles.

✝

It seemed there was quite the crustal deformation in the past five hundred years.

The research team had apparently found this underground structure on the first day, and its present condition was vastly different from the way it used to be. The walls and ceilings had caved in, unable to withstand the twisting ground around them, and the original hallways had been sealed up only to create new ones. There were gaps here and there in the outer wall, and the soil and water made the pathways even more difficult to navigate.

They followed the paths down, relying on the faint light the small illumination crystal produced. As Willem watched Glick proceed without hesitation through the interweaving paths ahead of him, he sensed his genuine dignity as a seasoned salvager.

His breath came out in white clouds. The air was as frigid as that of an ice room.

With every level they went down, the temperature dropped, too. They came to the fourth level belowground. Water dripping in from a nearby water vein pooled on the floor and froze on the spot. They had to be even more careful when they walked so they didn't slip.

"As you can tell by what you've already seen, most of the stuff on the surface has basically been weathered away, so it's not really good for treasure hunting. But here, underground, lots of stuff is still the way it used to be. The real salvaging happens once we dive in."

Willem paid no attention to Glick's commentary.

"This thing has at least four floors, and every floor is huge. Never thought this mazelike thing would be around my hometown."

He felt strange.

Maybe it had been here ever since he lived in the orphanage. Or maybe it was built after he left to become a Quasi Brave. Though now, five hundred years after the fact, there was no way to check.

"You all right back there?"

"Yeah, I'm fine."

When he turned to see how Chtholly was doing, she didn't seem to be having any particular trouble, even with the uneven footing in the dark. She was, after all, the girl recognized by Seniorious.

"—Oh yeah, the girls."

"Hmm?"

"It was just like you told me—they're good kids."

"Yeah."

Nopht and Rhantolk—Willem still didn't know them very well, but if Glick said so, and he'd been fraternizing with them for a while now, then it was probably true.

Willem somehow felt like Glick had gotten ahead of him, and he felt a bit salty.

"I'm not giving 'em to you."

"Hey, c'mon, where did that come from?"

They cackled together.

"If they want, then you're gonna have to go through me first."

"Seriously, where did that come from? And you really need to cut it out with that serious look on your face. It's creeping me out."

"What on earth are you two talking about?" Chtholly smiled slightly, exasperated.

A puff of white breath floated in the cool air of the underground and vanished.

"—Wait, hold on. The way's blocked."

Willem saw the back of Glick's head stop moving in the small field of vision provided by the lighting crystal.

He narrowed his eyes and peered at the path ahead of them. He could see a small pile of debris of all shapes and sizes. Even if they wanted to break it to keep going, putting any unnecessary pressure on it might cause the ceiling to collapse.

"Damn. I guess we came all this way just to head back."

"There were plenty of side routes on the way here, though, right? Can't we go around?"

"The paths are too mixed up. It would take too much time to study each and every one. And there's also a Timere nest around here; I don't wanna just walk aimlessly and irritate them."

"I guess so." Willem thought for a moment. "A what nest?"

"Timere, Beast Number Six." Glick spoke lightly. "About ten of 'em get together and build their nests in the ground. They usually just sleep like regular plants when they're in their nests, but that's why if you wander nearby unguarded, they'll wake up and attack you, even if that's only in really rare cases."

Number Six, Timere—the only Beast that could get to Regule Aire by drifting in the air. The very reason why the disposable weapons that were the faeries existed.

—Why don't we just burn 'em all now?

The question almost made its way out of Willem's mouth, but he quickly swallowed it. They had to drag out Carillons against them because they weren't enemies that could be dealt with by such simple methods.

Then should they make Nephren and the others attack now, while they knew their chances of a sneak attack were almost guaranteed?

No, they couldn't. It was out of the question. They were in an enclosed space, where they would have to completely abandon their advantage of having wings. Tens of Beasts had even more duplication power, making for a depressing difference in number. When faced with these realities, it wasn't actually that advantageous to surprise attack them.

The one good point was the enclosed space and high density of enemies meant favorable conditions for the "self-destruct" that was the faeries' final attack. He didn't want to think about actually executing it, though.

"…Er, do you mind?"

Willem heard Chtholly's voice and snapped back to reality.

"I don't really know how to explain my reasoning, but…can we go in through this path?"

Since they wouldn't have accomplished anything if they turned back now, they decided to give the path a go.

They traversed along the twisting, winding path for what seemed like forever. Whenever there was a fork in the road, Chtholly would stop, strain her ears, then pick one of the paths without a moment's hesitation.

"I don't know how to explain it, but it feels like someone's calling me."

That was how she expressed it. It wasn't entirely reliable as a compass for people trying to push their way deep into a natural labyrinth. But since they didn't have anything else to guide them at the moment, there was really no reason for them to stop her.

It was almost impossible to tell how long they had been walking.

They arrived at a room, and their vision opened up before them.

"…For real?" Glick murmured in admiration. "We made it. This is what I wanted to show you."

"Huh?" Willem spun around, looking at his surroundings. "There's nothing here, man. What did you want to show me?"

"It's in front of you."

Despite what he said, the only thing in front of them was a wall.

No, wait. On closer inspection, it wasn't a wall but a giant block of ice.

"Almost the entire room was encased in ice at first, but I've managed to work my way this far." Glick lightly tapped the block of ice with his knuckle.

There was something in the ice.

Willem raised the illumination crystal up to it.

He could see a brilliant crimson color inside the unnaturally transparent ice.

He gulped.

"…This is…"

"Surprised, eh? I was, too. Never thought I'd find treasure like this twice in my short life."

It was a young child—young even when compared to the little ones at the faerie warehouse.

Her hair was a long crimson, frozen in place as though it had been fluttering gently in the wind.

It was hard to see her expression, but she looked to be resting peacefully.

And in her chest…

…was a gaping sword wound.

She looked alive. She looked like she was just in a serene slumber. But there was no mistaking that this was a corpse.

"She's not…an acquaintance from long ago or anything, is she?"

"Uhhh…" He checked her face again. "I don't think so."

"Okay. It was a lot like the time when I found you, so I just thought, maybe, you know?"

Right. This situation wasn't the first time for Glick. Willem was once hidden away so elaborately—petrified, sunk in water, then encased in ice. It was Glick and his other salvager buddies who'd picked him up and revived him.

"Could you save her like you did me?"

"I don't think that's possible." Glick shook his head slightly. "In your case, you were petrified because of a curse, so we could save you because you weren't totally dead yet. No matter how you look at it, this kid's just plain old dead."

That was true. There wasn't a single emnetwiht who could live with a heart cut in two.

"Just hold on a second."

Willem activated a slight bit of venenum and gave his eyes Sight.

"…Yeah, I thought so."

"Hmm?"

"There's some kind of curse on the wound."

He gazed steadily at it, enduring the throbbing pain in his head. He could clearly see a strong curse deeply carved into the small body.

"Seriously?"

"Seriously. It doesn't seem like something that'll bring her back to life if we lift it, though."

The world contained curses meant to be cast on dead bodies. Those were the kind that made corpses move to put them to work, or only made the mouth move to spew wisdom, or to create ties with its blood relatives to infect them with the curse—things like that. And of course, by lifting them, the cursed corpses would just become uncursed corpses. They wouldn't be brought back to life.

"…Hmm?"

That aside, he thought he'd seen this curse somewhere before.

He looked closer. This was probably a kind of orthodox transmutation curse—the kind that turned people into frogs or a delicious meal into stone. Something about how the power entwined and twisted with things—stuff like that. But he couldn't remember where he'd seen it before. Either way, his pounding headache was preventing him from making a coherent thought.

He stopped the Sight. His headache wasn't going away anytime soon.

"I wanted to put her to rest in a brighter place, instead of letting her sleep in this creepy hole… But I guess if she's cursed, then should we lift that first?"

Glick was mumbling about something.

"What, you're not gonna sell it off as a treasure to some creepy collector?"

"I'm not really into that kind of stuff. She seems so comfortable resting now, so I just want to do the compassionate thing and let her rest."

Somehow, when Glick said *compassionate*, that convinced him.

Willem turned back to the girl.

"Well, whatever we decide to do, we've got to get her out of this ice first. This kinda curse keeps the victim semi-permanently fixed. So she probably won't rot or get eaten even if we take her out of the—"

*   *   *

First, a shiver ran down his spine.

"—Huh?"

A moment afterward, a baseless sense of fear bubbled up from deep inside his gut. As though he was being propelled into action, he looked for the source. He whirled around. He found it immediately.

Chtholly stood there in astonishment, gazing at the girl in the ice.

He could *see* the storm of venenum quietly overflowing throughout her whole body.

"Wha...?"

Her hair began to change color before his very eyes.

From blue to red—Chtholly Nota Seniorious was vanishing.

"What the hell?! What are you *doing*?!"

He gripped her shoulders and shook her. He smacked her cheeks several times. But the kindled venenum did not subside. Her gaze was not fixed on any particular thing, and it was hard to tell if she was even conscious. Willem understood that if he didn't do something *now*, it would already be too late. He made his palm in the shape of a wedge, and pierced the spot beside Chtholly's heart as hard as he could.

An expression of agony briefly crossed the girl's face. Her blood flow was agitated, her lungs crushed, her activated venenum forcefully scattered, and her fuzzy consciousness forcibly shut off.

"Sorry, talk later! We have to go back up, now!"

"O-okay."

Though Glick sounded hesitant, he must have seen how the situation had changed. Glick nodded obediently and immediately led them back on the path they had come from.

3. The Tattered, Antiquated Clock

The next day.

Just as announced, the first officer went underground with a big group of thirteen Guardsmen in tow. The ones left behind were now forced to continue with their original loading work, even without the manpower of thirteen people.

They returned much earlier than sunset.

"See, not a single lick of danger down there!" the first officer boasted. Either the thirteen he'd brought along were exceptionally skilled, or they brought results back that warranted such boasting.

By the way, let's talk a little bit about Beast Number Six, the Deeply Buried Timere.

They are typically amorphous. They also grow and divide quickly. Though the chances of it happening are extremely rare, they are the only Beast that can be encountered in the sky.

When they're not in the sky, the creatures make nests underground. They find caves that are relatively spacious and damp, attach themselves firmly to the walls and ceilings, and slowly increase their numbers.

As for how terrifying Sixes' nests seem, they're sometimes not actually all that dangerous. There are more than a few stories of salvagers getting lost smack in the middle of their nests only to return home unharmed. Nesting Sixes don't respond to only one or two intruders. They stay dormant, almost as though they're still asleep.

It is unknown what causes them to come alive.

There are actually some people who think that's impossible. They think Sixes are completely irrational, running about causing havoc without any regard for the races of Regule Aire, spreading tragedy wherever they want. There is no point in thinking why or when they are awake or asleep, since that is their nature.

But in reality, that train of thought is wrong.

Though it isn't for certain, there are several conditions that act as keys to undoing their slumber. For example, if a whole group of living creatures gets close enough. Then, when one or more conditions are met, several nesting Sixes will slowly wake from their sleep and begin to act, looking for living victims.

*   *   *

A small hole popped open on the sandy surface as the unrelenting wind washed over it.

And then, another one.

And after that, another one.

And another one, and another one, and another one.

And another one, and another one, and another one. And another one, and another one, and another one. And another one, and another one, and another one. And another one, and another one, and another one. And another one, and another one, and another one. And another one, and another one, and another one. And another one, and another one, and another one.

It was like a spring of water.

Slowly, a liquefied substance oozed out from each hole.

They said that in the ancient language of the emnetwiht, *timere* meant "a fearful or anxious heart." The concept was that it bubbled up from everywhere; grew unnoticed; and, before one was aware, gnawed at the heart, crushed it, and devoured everything.

There was no way to know now why one of the Seventeen Beasts came to be crowned with that word. It might have been that the old scholars gave it the name on their gut feeling without really thinking about it. But regardless of the particulars, there they were, the very embodiment of that feeling.

A countless number of Beast Number Sixes, Timere, rose from beneath the sand.

†

As it so happens, there was a tattered, old, anachronistic clock hanging on the wall of the ship's hold. Its frame was warped from the humidity, and the wires on its hands were twisted. It was a staunch thing, said to have already been worn down even when the oldest serving crew members first came on the ship.

They say it was a keepsake that belonged to the ship's first captain's grandmother. And the story of how it came to hang on the ship's wall was one that no one could listen to without shedding a tear... But not a single person had ever heard the details of the story. Someone had probably made that up.

The tattered clock was just a tattered clock. It was useful in that one could look up and see the current time. It was nothing more, nothing less.

At the time, the clock's hands pointed to six and twenty-six.

The first victim was a strapping young ailuanthrope, unluckily charged with cleaning the windows. With an old mop in one hand, he was in the middle of desperately trying to scrub away at the sand that stuck to the window frame.

He didn't even have a spare moment to scream.

At the time, the clock's hands pointed to six and twenty-eight.

A somewhat tipsy lizardfolk third officer was walking down the corridor when he heard a grating *bang, bang, bang* coming from the window. Wondering what it was, he went over to look, and he saw something dark green stuck to the other side of the window. And somehow, it looked like the green mass was trying to forcibly push its way through the window—no, the ship's hull itself.

The third officer screamed.

A large crack spread across the window.

At the time, the clock's hands pointed to six and thirty-two.

There was an explosive sound, and the furnaces began to whir.

They had to get away from the ground as fast as possible. Otherwise, everything they had would be swallowed up by the gray sand and vanish.

"Wh...wh-wh-wh-what is that?!" the bewildered first officer cried, and

Glick looked out the window in turn. Beyond the faint sandstorm, the silhouettes of countless treelike forms extended their trunks and stretched their branches as they tried to ensnare the body of the *Plantaginesta*.

"Whaddaya mean? That's a swarm of Sixes," Glick grumbled in response as he stuffed cannonballs one at a time into a large cannon.

There was no way, of course, that a cannon could kill any of the Seventeen Beasts, but if it went well enough, then they could at least intimidate them. At the very least, it would be much better than doing nothing at all.

"Y-you think it's okay that we turn on the engines? I heard that's how *Saxifraga* ended up falling!"

That was because *Saxifraga* had been up against Beast Four. It relied on sound and movement to search for prey. The low humming of the furnaces would have been like painting a target on their forehead.

But Timere wasn't like that. Whether they had a good sense of sight or smell or whatever it might be, they unerringly searched out the living and attacked. It didn't matter if their prey held their breath or pretended to be dead or hid behind a door. As long as they were alive, they could not run from their fangs or their claws or whatever they had.

But on the flip side, that also meant that even if an inanimate object, like a furnace, made the biggest sounds in the world and moved erratically all over the place, it would not catch Timere's interest.

There was no time to be explaining all these little details, and it probably wouldn't matter anyway.

"Where are those dug weapons?! They're here for times like these, aren't they?! Hurry and make them clean up!!"

"Don't make others deal with the problems you brought on yourself when you decided to ignore reality!"

The ship's body shuddered violently. It tipped. The propellers spun wildly fast in desperation.

The ground rose.

"Okay, we'll keep altitude at the fastest possible speed and shake off as many stuck to the outer hull as we can! We'll get the ladies to do their work after that!"

There was a hopeless thudding sound coming from the outer walls. It somehow almost sounded like it was getting closer.

"Some of them've gotten inside! Evacuate everyone to a safe place!"

"I—I can't do that! I'm an officer, not a—not a commander! This is outside my expertise!"

"Oh yeah?"

If the officer was abandoning his work, then that made things easier for Glick. He grabbed the microphone and began yelling orders to all broadcasting devices throughout the ship. Of course, he didn't have any expertise or anything like that, either, but in a situation like this, someone who could do *something* had to do it, otherwise no one would survive.

The clock's hands pointed to six and thirty-four.

Chtholly wasn't waking up.

She had showed no signs of opening her eyes after she fainted underground.

They immediately ran back to the airship afterward and rushed to the infirmary. They grabbed the hired doctor and asked him to do something, *anything* to wake her up.

But of course, in the end, nothing worked.

It wasn't like she'd fallen ill or had any obvious flesh wounds in the first place. There wasn't any treatment for someone with no visible abnormalities. She did actually have a long, thin bit of internal bleeding in her chest, but that probably didn't have anything to do with her coma.

Willem sat on the floor beside Chtholly as she slept, his head in his hands.

There was no point in repairing Lapidemsibilus at this juncture, now that her condition had come to this. That Carillon preserved the health of the user's body and mind to the best of its ability. It wouldn't work if its own user never activated even the smallest bit of venenum to awaken the sword.

"…What am I doing?" he groaned quietly.

He wanted to make her happy.

He *knew* he wanted to make her happy.

How much had he done for her ever since she woke up?

How much had he done to steer her in the direction of the future she wanted?

He couldn't think of a single thing.

(*—You don't really think much of her at all, do you?*)

A voice whispered to him from a dark place deep in his heart.

(*You were concerned about her because she was Seniorious's user. You never paid any mind to Chtholly herself. The only one you ever wanted to save was Lillia. The only promise you ever wanted to keep was the one you made with Almaria. Neither went very well at all, so since Chtholly's situation was similar, you got caught up with her to fool yourself.*)

No.

He had been looking at Chtholly for who she was.

(*You realized you could* never *make her happy, didn't you? Seniorious's choice itself is like a curse. Her ability to wield it means from start to finish, she's been bound, whether by fate or destiny or whatever. She never had a way out to begin with.*)

No. No. No.

She could have been happy. That's what he'd intended to give her.

(*She was always being saved on the excuse that she's a kid, right? You never looked at her for who she was. You kept your distance between the two of you. You might have embraced her, but she never embraced* you. *You were always the one to give her things, and she never gave you anything in return. She didn't even stir the order of important things in your heart.*)

No. No. No. No. No. No. No.

I—I just… She—she was…

(*"I tried my hardest to do everything I could! But I just couldn't defy fate! It's not my fault! Fate is all there is to blame!"* …*If it's fate you're up against, then everyone will pity you. No one's gonna blame you. Oh, right, that's 'cause there was nothing wrong with what you did. But—*)

No—

(*—what was totally fine for you ended up being fatally wrong for someone else.*)

The airship rolled.

Glick was yelling over the announcement system for all personnel to seek shelter.

Willem listened vacantly, the words going in one ear and out the other.

"...'Marry me,' huh?"

Those were the words that came out of his mouth the day before.

"...What do I really think of her...?"

He stood slowly.

He lightly pressed his own lips against Chtholly's as she slept.

Plop. A single teardrop brimmed in his eye and spilled onto her cheek.

He stepped back.

He could hear the grating sound of metal being split open. It sounded like the intruders had entered the ship from the outside, somewhere not too far from his location.

"...Ha-ha."

He gave a small laugh and turned his back to Chtholly.

Though oblivious intruders they were, he was a little thankful for them. He could spend his time much better than just sitting here, thinking about awful things.

"Sorry. I'll be back in a sec."

That was all he said as he spoke over his shoulder and left the room.

The clock's hands pointed to six and thirty-five.

The outlook of the battle was grim.

But for Rhantolk, there were two things she felt grateful for.

One was that since there were a great number of attacking Timere, the individual size of each Timere was not that big. Any attempt on their lives would not outright kill them. More appropriately, they divided just before their moment of death to double their selves, then they pushed the state of "death" onto one half, and the other half lived on. This repeated until each individual reached its division limit. The good thing was that, in essence, she did not see larger individual bodies among them whose division limit would be above ten. Just ten divisions meant even a lone faerie could kill them if she worked hard enough.

The other good thing was how light her body felt. Her venenum had never kindled so readily before, and it easily poured into her sword, Historia. So much so that she almost forgot how serious the situation was; it almost felt refreshing. She knew why— It was that "treatment" Second Officer Willem Kmetsch had done with his hand. She had doubted him, thinking he had simply pressed about randomly because he just wanted to touch young female bodies, but it seemed she was wrong. He certainly was amazing. Personality-wise...she found him favorable, which also meant that he was the type she wanted to tease. She could see how Chtholly was infatuated with him. If he wasn't an emnetwiht, of all things, she might even fancy him.

"Num...ber...Three...!"

She finished off one Beast.

She flapped her wings straightaway and put distance between herself and the Beasts clinging to the side of the *Plantaginesta*. The Beasts could not fly. As long as she stayed in the air with her faerie wings, then she could keep a certain degree of battlefield dominance.

And the *Plantaginesta* would soon secure a good altitude. The Beasts clung to one another, forming a ladder with their bodies as they tried to clamber up, but they were quickly reaching their limit and falling back to the land.

"Okay..."

Now their reinforcements from the ground were gone. All that was left was to clean up the creatures already clinging to the side of the ship.

She looked out over the *Plantaginesta* again.

The lower third of the ship was completely enwrapped in Timere, almost as though it were prey that had fallen into a leech-infested swamp. Though she didn't want to look right at them, she still couldn't ignore them, and she counted roughly a hundred or two hundred of them.

"...No, no. It can't be *roughly* a hundred, can it?" She unwittingly murmured a complaint about her own calculations.

Even if the division limit for one body was a sensible number, it was ridiculous how hopeless it was, with how many individual bodies there were in the first place. Even though she was now in good condition from having her venenum poisoning or whatnot cured, a long, strenuous battle right afterward would just make her worse again.

Even with a few favorable factors, the outlook of the battle was still unbelievably grim.

The clock's hands pointed to six and thirty-eight.

Rejoice, for this is the battlefield.
Something inside Willem whispered to him.

The battlefield was a place meant for the heroic to display their bravery. A place to fight against something, destroy something, and win something. A space born and spent for that process. Here there was excitement. Glory. Tragedy. Fantasy. Reality.

He once vied for the power to stand on the battlefield. He was once bitter because he couldn't. His heart was once pained when he sent those precious to him off to this place. So this moment now was something he should have long hoped for. It should have been a blessed, heart-stirring moment.

Was that always what he wanted? Had he always wanted to feel what it was like to knock down his enemies and win something among the pain?

"…Tch."

He clicked his tongue and brushed away the delusional distractions. He hunkered down and dashed through the corridor.

A gray mass suddenly flew at him from his side, striking at him about waist height. He lowered himself down even more and let it pass over his head.

The corridor itself became sliced—no, smashed to bits. The overwhelming mass and speed practically made him laugh. Its destructive power was almost hilarious. Bolts and screws and copper and steel plates—metal bits of all shapes and sizes danced in the air. A piece that someone had graffitied flew by in the corner of his vision. *May Regule Aire always stay at peace.*

The thing slipped from between the cracks in the wall to show itself. It was a gray crustacean. Its sturdy-looking shell and joints made it look a little like a crab. But of course, real crabs didn't have ten or more legs, and those legs didn't expand and contract.

It looked like a monster. It was easy to tell.

—*This must be a Seventeen Beast thing.*

He'd heard a lot about them, but it was his first time seeing one.

He thought he might find himself overcome by deep emotion, but he didn't really feel anything in particular. In front of him was just a deformed enemy with formidable power. That was all.

—*This might be the shadow of what was once emnetwiht.*

The possibility stirred something inside Willem ever so slightly. Just slightly.

Once emnetwiht? So what? This thing was in front of him now as a monster. And it was threatening them. That was all. That was enough.

A strong gust of wind howled from beyond the broken wall.

Three of the Beast's legs each flexed. It rushed at Willem to destroy him, mangling the ceiling and the walls and the floor as it did.

Willem slowly collapsed, closing the distance between himself and the Beast with a graceful step. It was the first step of the running style passed down through the bards in West Garmando. At its peak, it was a special move that would turn the body into shimmering hot air and send everything flying, but for the talentless Willem, he could use it for nothing more than a little distracting trick. And that was enough. The Beast moved and acted like a literal beast. It was nothing but formidable, and without techniques, it had no skills. Just by moving in a way to make it question its reality, he could easily dodge all its attacks.

He came right up to the side of the Beast, just a hairbreadth away. The surface of its body up close appeared to have some sort of odd-looking slime on it.

(I sure hope that ain't poison.)

He came to the conclusion as he pulled out his left fist. His fist made contact with a metal sheet that fell from the ceiling and smashed it right into the root of the Beast's leg. That didn't damage it, of course. He was up against something notorious for its ability to withstand concentrated artillery fire, so there was no way his bare fist would put it on its back.

He dropped. He bent his ankle. He turned his shoulders. He pooled all his breath into his stomach.

All of his movements tied together seamlessly and created a great strength that fed right into his fist.

The blow made a direct hit. If performed by a master, it was a technique said to have split mountains and caused waterfalls to flow backward, the question of whether that was fact or fiction aside. But those without experience, like Willem, could not pull off such a feat. The best he could do was push the opponent he punched a tiny bit forward.

And, of course, that was enough.

He pushed it toward a big gap in the wall; it was a gap that one of the Beast's legs had just created. And once it was thrown out into the air, the wingless Beast would no longer have any way to get back to the battlefield.

The Beast fell silently, wordlessly through the madder-red sky, slowly being swallowed up by the gray earth below. As he watched it go, he relaxed the alert tension throughout his body.

"...Gh—"

He'd pushed too hard with his broken body. Everywhere ached. He couldn't help but grimace.

He wrapped his arms around himself, checking for the damage. He was fine—as long as he didn't have any broken bones, then his precious muscles and tendons were intact. He could still move. He could still fight.

He could still stay on the battlefield. A bloodthirsty smile spread across his face.

"—I'm surprised."

Willem turned around, and he saw the color indigo fluttering in the violent wind.

"Hey, glad to see you're all right, Rhantolk." He gave a slight chuckle.

"I hate to say this, but it's thanks to you... It doesn't seem like you're doing all right, though," Rhantolk said, her face sour. "You're being too reckless. A wounded individual fighting with a Beast empty-handed, without using any venenum, *and* winning against it? What sort of joke is this?"

"What, you were watching? How embarrassing."

"No need to play dumb about it. You certainly are exasperat— Oh—"

Willem suddenly lost consciousness. The strength in his knees evaporated, and he started toppling in the direction of the hole in the wall. Just as he was about to soar through the air after the Beast, Rhantolk grabbed him, wrapped her arms around him, and collapsed back onto (what used to be) the corridor floor.

"Sorry." Willem's consciousness came right back. "You seriously saved me there."

"I certainly did. You should at least thank me. Can you stand?"

He checked himself. The answer was no—he had no strength left in his knees.

"Oh well. I suppose we'll take a little break. I'm a little tired, too, anyway," Rhantolk said as she straightened her posture.

She snuggled up to him, practically cradling his head in her bosom.

"H-hey!"

He was at a loss. Compared to Nephren, who always snuggled up to him in a similar fashion, Rhantolk's physique was just a little more on the— "I hope you're not having naughty thoughts." *Quit reading my mind.*

"Ha. You think I get excited over every kid I see?" He snorted, his question also acting as a means to convince himself.

"I see. I won't pursue the question of whether you actually mean that or if it's the result of self-control, but I appreciate it either way," she said as though seeing through his schemes, and she tightened her arms around him.

His ear was pressed hard against her slight chest. He could hear the sound of her heartbeat clear as day.

"...Your pulse is all over the place."

"I wasn't as reckless as you, but I did push myself a little too much earlier."

Venenum used the heart's power to spark. The reaction to such ferocity immediately manifested itself as an agitated heartbeat and blood flow. There was no questioning that this kind of intense arrhythmia was the result of the constant burning of venenum for battle without any regard for the future.

"You wouldn't happen to be able to use that odd technique of yours to fix it now, would you?"

No. Willem, who'd only really dabbled in it on the battlefield before, couldn't pull off dazzling feats like directly curing abnormalities in the heart with his treatment technique. He shook his head.

"You're more useless than I thought."

"...Than you thought? That means you were expecting more of me, huh?"

"Not at a—" She cut herself off to think for a moment. "...Actually, perhaps I was. I don't consider you trustworthy or reliable, but somewhere deep down, I was expecting something from you."

She sounded like a lizard he knew once. That didn't make him happy.

"Do you know how the battle's going? How are Nopht and Nephren doing?"

"I don't know exactly how many enemies there were, but there must be about ten or so left. I saw Nopht a little while ago from far away, and she seemed fine, but she was pushing herself as hard as I had been. I haven't seen Nephren yet, but she must be fighting down near the cargo hold."

"Okay."

He thought for a moment. The battle was clearly going poorly. The faeries were powerful, and there was no way they would fall behind in a one-on-one with these little grain-like Beasts. But the faeries were outnumbered and couldn't catch breaks when they wanted, so the longer the battle went on, the more at a disadvantage they would be.

"...I guess I—"

"Overruled."

The words he began to murmur were immediately stamped out.

"I haven't said anything yet."

"You looked like you were about to say something utterly nonsensical. I know what you're thinking. Since this isn't a situation where opening the gates to the faerie homeland won't solve anything, you would sacrifice yourself, become stone, and solve everything nicely. That way, there would be the least amount of losses—that's what you were thinking, wasn't it?"

I thought I told you not to read my mind.

"If not, then that wouldn't explain that big, happy grin on your face."

...

Oh. Guess that's the kind of face I was making.

"But for you, wouldn't it be a bit of a relief without me around?"

"I won't deny that. But I am not very fond of the thought of someone using their friends as an excuse to commit suicide."

Chtholly wasn't waking up. Willem was trying to throw himself into a desperate fight. It seemed that these two things were pretty obviously connected, even when viewed from the outside.

"Yeah, guess you're right."

He placed the palm of his hand on Rhantolk's head as she sat propping herself up. A disgusted look crossed her face, and she swatted him away. Well, of course she would.

"The number of enemies is dwindling. You should take a little rest. I'm gonna go check on the hold."

"Is that an order?"

"Take it as you like," Willem responded and ran off.

The clock's hands pointed to six and fifty-one.

"Gah!!"

With a powerful blow, Nopht went flying. She ricocheted off the walls and ceiling as she ripped pipes from their fixtures, rolled all the way to the end of the corridor, then finally stopped.

"Ngh…"

She'd just barely managed to give herself protection with her magic.

She didn't have any obvious wounds on her. But the impact left her right arm numb, and she could no longer move it.

"Ah-ha...ha-ha. Man, this is pretty bad."

She fixed her gaze on the Beast as it slowly approached, standing with shaky legs.

Keeping one's venenum constantly activated without any breaks was almost like running at full speed for the same amount of time. So the time Nopht was being forced straight into one battle after another was pushing her very close and very quickly to her limit.

But it was worth it. The number of enemies was waning. It wouldn't be very long before this grueling battle would be over. They would make it be over.

It would be done, and they would win—then what would happen?

The clock's hands pointed to six and fifty-ni—

A large hole opened up through the layers of steel plating plastered on the wall of the ship's hull.

The ship reeled.

The clock slipped from the wall. With a small *crack*, the clock face split.

The broken clock would never count the hours again.

Anyone would immediately be able to tell that Nephren's movements were slowing.

All the noncombatant personnel—basically, everyone besides the faeries—were taking shelter in the hold. The Beasts were gathering one after another to kill them. She was going to stop them and chase them away.

Her battle was one of endurance, staying in one place.

All elements of the location were working against her. Small-framed Nephren had very little stamina, and she never had the experience of maintaining concentration in a battle of one-on-many for an extended period of time. Since the main playing field ended up being in an enclosed space, she couldn't use her small frame or wings for mobility. Her sword, Insania, was large and heavy, but regardless, it was still inferior to the reach that the Beasts' tentacles had. Whenever she went to take her enemy's life, all she could do was slowly grind away at her own strength and concentration as she threw herself at it.

As time passed, the vitality in Nephren's actions dwindled, and the Beasts' numbers and drive grew. The line of battle had regressed, and they were now pushed back almost to the center of the hold. Then—

"If ya can't fly, you better grab on to somethin' quick—!"

Glick yelled over the announcement system from the control room, and as he pulled down several position-control tubes, he cut off the steering wheel. Being forced into an impossible action, the body of the ship gave a shrill cry. The bow of the ship tilted upward. The stern drooped downward.

All the Timere that had gathered in the hold in pursuit of living creatures silently slid down across the floor. In time with their movements, Nephren smashed out the large service door in the hold with her sword. All the things stuffed inside—rations for the trip home and spoils from the surface—flew out into space one after the other. The Beasts each transformed their tentacles and tried to cling onto the floor and walls, but the falling boxes pushed them out, and they, too, began falling to the ground.

One split its body into two as it fell. One half became a spring, and the other half made a huge leap off it. Its claw extended, about to grab onto Nephren, who lost balance.

"No way!"

One of the crew members threw a barrel of oil that had caught onto one of the beams. It was probably meant to be nothing more than a feint, but it luckily made a direct hit on the Beast, splattering a low-viscosity cooking oil everywhere. The claw was about to pierce Nephren's stomach, but it missed its mark and ended up only hitting the back of her head lightly. The Beast transformed its tentacles into that of a thorny crustacean and tried to cling to the floor. But it was slick with oil, and the Beast couldn't support its own weight. Soon, that Beast, too, joined its brethren and was flung out into the open sky. All the crew members cheered.

"You did it, little missy!"

Someone sent a cheer of appreciation Nephren's way. At that moment—

Slip.

Nephren's body began to slide across the tilted floor.

She had breached her limits. She had been fighting on willpower alone. The last blow she received from the Beast and the relief that she'd success-fully kept the hold safe for now was enough to snip the last thread of her willpower.

"No!!"

Several crew members raised their voices in a cry. Some of them crawled along the floor to get closer, but Nephren gazed up at them with a hazy look.

"...Stay...away."

Her body was burning. But, at the same time, cold as ice.

She'd burned up too much of her venenum. She'd overused the power, born from turning her back to her life and taking a step closer to death without thinking about what would come after. And so, there was only one destination waiting for her after this.

Overdrive. Then, the rampaging waves of energy would blow away anything and everything around it. It was an overwhelming yet absolute display of power, strong enough to easily render even the largest of Timere to nothing.

"Just wait, I'll be right there!"

A frogger crew member plastered his fingers against the floor, moving slowly toward her.

She couldn't let this happen. She couldn't let them save her. It was that thought alone that put her body into motion.

"What are you doing?!"

She lightly pushed off from the floor.

Nephren jumped into the wide-open sky that connected them to the ground—and fell.

✝

From the corner of his eye and beyond the rip in the outer wall, Willem saw an unconscious Nephren falling.

"Wha…?"

His mind went blank. In the next moment, he was already flying through the roaring, whirling wind.

His eyes were screaming in pain, but he forced them open and followed Nephren's figure. She was falling backward, Insania no longer in her hands, unable to make any movement of her own.

Then, her surroundings. The Beasts that must've fallen from the ship before Nephren were awkwardly trying to ride the wind to get closer to her.

This isn't funny.

With that one thought, he decided to give up on everything.

He used the Nightingale Sweep. He kicked off the air and flew to Insania's hilt. He activated his venenum. He clenched his jaw to ignore the shocks of pain that ran all throughout his body as he tried to wake the Carillon through its hilt. He couldn't. Willem Kmetsch didn't have the skill to use high-level Carillon.

That didn't discourage him. Because he'd known that from the very beginning.

Fighting against the ferocity of the storm-like wind resistance, he reached up with his left hand to the center of the blade.

"Initialize…adjustment…!!"

Insania's blade split into pieces. The cracks widened, and light filled the gaps between them.

In its splintered state, Willem reached out to the crystal fragment that made up Insania's core and forcefully pulled it toward him. The veins of enchantment ripped and frayed. The spinal root was no longer able to circulate the power, and it began to heat up, unable to stand against the pressure inside it.

The Carillon Insania was already gone. All that remained was a raging clump of power that once used to be a Carillon.

"Leave her—"

There were thirteen Beasts in total after Nephren.

And in a few more seconds, they would impact with the ground and die.

"—the hell...*alone*...!!"

He performed a second Nightingale Sweep, then the draconic festering. He let loose a monstrous roar and attacked the horde of Beasts.

4. The Happiest Girl in the World

By the time she realized it, the girl stood in a dark ruin.

Before her stood a child, one she felt like she'd seen somewhere before, tears welling in her eyes.

—*What's wrong, Elq?*

The girl's memory was hazy, but she somehow remembered the child's name.

Did you have a bad dream?

Elq's body shivered.

"...*Chtholly*..."

Elq looked up at the girl and murmured someone's name. Whose name was it? It sounded familiar. She thought for a moment.

Ah, right. That was "my" name. The girl accepted the name, feeling as though she was seeing an old friend for the first time in a long time. Now that she was hearing it again, it was a weird name. It was hard to remember, hard to say, and not very cute.

"*I'm sorry.*"

Why are you apologizing?

"*I knew this would happen. I knew there were so many bad things.*"

Now that I think about it, that's right. It's okay.

Actually, I should thank you. It's thanks to you, thanks to how you closed your eyes for me, that I could keep my promises. I could go home to where I wanted.

It seems like I lost a lot along the way, though.

"...*Chtholly?*"

I do have one request.

But this is probably my last.

"But..."

I can't really remember the details, but there's someone I want to help.

There are feelings I want to express. So please.

"No matter what?"

No matter what.

"You won't come back this time, Chtholly."

I'm almost completely gone anyway.

And—I finally understand. Was that what "I" really was in the first place?

Is that the real reason why Seniorious chose me?

"..."

I understand everything. That is why I'm asking you.

Please— Just one last time. Let me go back.

She slowly pushed herself up.

The girl with long red hair got up from bed.

"Umm..."

Where was she? Who was she?

As though her mind were enshrouded in mist—no, completely covered in mud—she couldn't remember a thing.

There was a deep vibrating sound, and the world shook. She could hear the loud sounds of metal clashing against metal from far away. She thought absently to herself—this must be some kind of battlefield.

She found the door and wandered out of the room. She came to a cramped and narrow corridor.

She walked around the area without any particular destination. She finally came across a spot with a strangely nice view. Most of the wall had been pulled off, and outside she could see a wide blue sky as the sun set.

The deep cerulean changed to a light purple, slowly being taken over by red.

"Chtholly...?"

There was a groaning voice, and she turned around.

A girl was collapsed in the dingy corridor, her arms and legs splayed out in all directions. Her entire body was injured so badly she couldn't move, despite how extremely agitated her venenum seemed.

"You idiot, it's dangerous out here... Now that you're awake, you needa go hide somewhere."

Is she an acquaintance? she thought.

It sounded like this girl knew who she was. But she couldn't remember who the girl was at all. That piece of her heart had already vanished.

But there were more important things to think about. The sky spread wide before her on the other side of the large hole in the wall.

There she saw a silhouette, one that seemed on the verge of disappearing.

"Ah—"

She remembered. It was him. She couldn't recall his name, but he must have been someone so important to her.

It was just a hunch, but she had the feeling that he was the type to load unnecessary burden onto himself. But still, even so, why was he out there in a free fall? She had a feeling he wasn't the type of creature that had wings, so if he hit the ground with that much force, he would die.

"I suppose I've got no choice, do I?"

She stepped over the wrecked wall and jumped off, too—but not yet. There was a nice-looking sword on the ground next to her, and she picked it up. Its name was engraved on the hilt: Desperatio. Interesting— "Severed Hope" was the bluff in its name.

"No, don't go," the collapsed girl moaned. "Don't fight anymore. Don't end up a casualty here. We'll fight your share of the battle. That's why"— she paused to give a loud cough, perhaps from the lung damage—"if you don't have to fight, then don't. If you can find happiness, then be happy. None of us would accept it if you didn't." The girl's wandering gaze finally fixed on her, and she begged her. Her consciousness was probably hazy because of the overuse of venenum.

"I'm sorry. I will never be able to be happier than this."

She sent a slight amount of venenum through Desperatio. It melded smoothly with the blade, as though it was a part of her body to begin with.

"Because I finally realized that I have always been happy."

A broad, tooth-baring smile crossed her face.

And the girl leaped into the unending sky.

Her hair whipped around violently in the wind.

Her whole body was overflowing with venenum without her having to kindle any more.

Many books
burning as they fall.
A serpent swimming in flames.
The silver moon
crumbling to pieces.

Her soul fell to pieces with quiet *ding, ding*s audible only to herself.

One piece fell. And then another one.

A ship sailing
across the stars.
Rows of coffins, all lined up.
A cracked canopy.

Ding, ding, ding.

So many things slipped from her mind. All the fun times; all the bad times. She could feel her heart being erased, turning into a blank canvas. But—

"Good luck."

Her lips spontaneously bent into a smile.

He deeply regretted, from the bottom of his heart, that he never finished studying midair techniques. Well, it was obvious that the greater question was whether his talentless self could've produced good results in the first place, even if he'd studied them, but that was irrelevant right now. He just couldn't scratch away the feeling of *what if.*

He first cleared the area of Beasts as he clutched the unconscious Nephren. Now, he was currently supercharging all the venenum he could possibly activate so that most of it could bear the impact of their fall. Nevertheless, the shock battered Willem's whole body, one that could rip him into pieces and still not be enough.

With Nephren in his arms, he rolled far across the gray sand. The friction of the sand ripped and tore at his skin, rubbing away even further at the exposed blood and flesh.

"Rgh... Agh...!"

They stopped spinning. He coughed up a mass of air and blood from his crushed lungs.

His entire body was numb. Maybe he should be thankful for that. If he hadn't been paralyzed—if his pain receptors were fully functional—then he probably wouldn't be able to stay conscious. That was how bad Willem's wounds were.

(—Shit.)

He had ventured beyond the realm of desperation. He couldn't move and probably wouldn't ever again. But they weren't out of danger yet. All the Beasts he hadn't been able to fight off during the fall were slowly starting to lift themselves up from the dunes of sand. And he could tell the horde of Beasts left on the ground when the airship took off were silently closing the distance from far away. Their numbers were probably easily over a hundred.

(There has to be something. A way, anything.)

He barely managed to string together his consciousness, as it still felt like it could vanish at any moment, and forced himself to think like there was literally no tomorrow. But he thought of nothing. He could think of a hundred ways and a hundred outcomes, a thousand ways and a thousand outcomes, and they would all lead to their death.

(This isn't funny.)

He gritted his teeth, most of which were broken.

(I—I can't just give up on these kids' futures—)

"You saying you'll always be right by their side protecting them?"

He suddenly heard his master's snide remark from the back of his mind.

Shut up, go away, this isn't the time to be remembering you, he thought, but it didn't go away that easily.

"Ahhh—be glad, Quasi Brave. Because you can never become a Legal Brave."

...Right. He'd simply ignored it back then, but now he wondered what that meant. One needed a special background in order to become a Legal Brave. Whether it be birth or upbringing or destiny, Willem knew well that he had absolutely nothing to do with that kind of stuff. So then why had his master felt the need to say that to remind him all over again?

(—That doesn't matter right now!)

A Beast was drawing straight toward them. He wanted to counterattack, but he couldn't move a single finger.

This is it, huh?

A small seed of defeat sprouted in his heart. From that moment, his consciousness began to fade rapidly.

Sorry, Nephren. I couldn't protect you.

I'm sorry, Chtholly. I couldn't make you happy.

And, and—

It was the very last moment before his consciousness was completely swallowed by darkness.

He thought he saw someone land gently on the ground by their side.

5. The End of a Dream

It was like swimming in a dream.

A raring impatience clung incessantly to her limbs.

Time stretched out indefinitely. Her consciousness was accelerating.

Every single time she swung her right arm once, she lost two things.

A Beast evaporated, swallowed up by the raging inferno of venenum.

With quiet *ding, ding*s audible only to her, the pieces of "Chtholly" that were barely left in the girl were slowly chiseled away.

(—*Ahhh*—)

She must have had memories she never wanted to lose.

But she could no longer remember what those were.

She must have had futures she never wanted to give up on.

But she could no longer even picture what a future was.

She lost everything.

She let it all go.

She didn't regret it. At least, she didn't think so. Probably. She couldn't really tell. The memories to show her how to make that judgment were already gone.

How long had she spent doing that?

She thought the battle would be never ending, but it still came to a conclusion in the end.

The number of sliced, pummeled, burned Beasts was 715.

That was all of them.

She saw that all the Beasts in the area were no more, and she finally stopped.

The wind died down.

Her fiery red hair reflected the moonlight, shimmering softly.

Someone was collapsed on the ground.

Who is it? she thought.

She struggled to put her head to one side, then she looked over to them.

In the darkness of night, she saw a young man with black hair cradling a girl to his chest, both unconscious.

"Ah..."

She lifted her head, about to say something. But her throat had been completely worn out from her reckless breathing in the earlier battle, and she didn't even know what she would say in the first place.

The man's expression made him seem close to tears. For some reason, she thought that was sad.

Who was he?

He must have been someone incredibly dear and precious to her.

But she couldn't remember who he was.

She couldn't even feel a sense of loss.

I want him to laugh, she thought.

I want him to make that cheeky smile, she thought.

But at the same time, she also thought, *I want him to cry*.

She also desperately wished he would love her, the empty shell that she had become, so much so that she wanted to burst into tears. *I am terrible. I am truly, truly terrible.*

She thought she saw the young man just barely open his eyes and look at her. Joy burst from deep within her heart. Now, she could tell him. Even after her heart had lost everything else, even after she lost sight of who she was herself, the only thing that remained was her last wish.

There was something she wanted to tell him, no matter what, before she disappeared completely.

"Thank...you."

She managed to somehow move her lips to form the words.

In the end, she used all the strength she could muster to smile.

And this time, the girl's consciousness ceased for good.

The damage report was thick enough to be its own tome.

It wasn't entirely unheard of. The value of a large-size airship didn't start and stop with it just being a complicated machine. The detailed rights of which routes it could fly on and which ports it could dock at cost a bit of money themselves. And on top of that, if someone was considering flying it down to the surface, then the rights that must be purchased would out-number the number of fingers and toes on both hands and both feet (we're thinking about races with five fingers on one hand, five toes on one foot, and two hands and two feet, here).

That said, the correspondence sent to the faerie warehouse was simple.

It said: In the sudden battle that broke out at Ground Level K96, MAL Ruins, Second Officer Willem Kmetsch and his secretary went missing in action.

Additionally, the equipment listed below was lost in the battle:

Dug weapon Insania.

Dug weapon Desperatio.

Dug weapon compatible user, faerie soldier Nephren Ruq Insania.

Since Second Officer Kmetsch did not have any family, the compensation will be passed on to his workplace, the Orlandry Alliance Warehouse No. 4, and added to its operating fees, in accordance with his life's wishes—

Now But a Distant Dream—B
-la chanteuse-

This is a story from a little while ago.

When one girl was still very young, just after she was born.

On the outskirts of Island No. 94, in a deep and dark forest, the girl stood before a mossy stone monument, crying, *Waaah, waaah*. Her loud cries echoed throughout the forest as she continued her tempest of tears.

She was sad. She had no idea why, but a profound sense of loss continued to bubble from deep within her heart, and it didn't stop.

"Wow, that's loud!"

One faerie soldier, who had just finished a fight nearby, plugged her ears as she spoke with a smile.

"The feelings from her past life are really influencing her! This child must be pure!"

The other faerie soldier also plugged her ears to answer.

"You mean she's simple and easily swayed?!"

"You could say that!"

The two exchanged glances and approached the girl.

They stooped down to the girl's eye level and spoke to her softly.

"Good evening. How are you feeling?"

Waaah.

"...She's not listening."

"She probably *can't* hear, geez."

"This is what you're supposed to do in times like these!" one of the faerie soldiers announced as she grabbed the girl and forced her into a hug.

Children needed to breathe in order to bawl. So when their faces were pushed into someone's chest, they couldn't breathe very well. The girl stopped crying quickly, began to flail her arms and legs about, then suddenly stopped.

"Good, that's settled."

"...Are you sure she's not dead?"

"She was just tired and fell asleep. Look."

They both strained their ears to hear again, and they heard soft snoring—it was almost impossible to think how loudly she had been bawling only moments earlier. The wind swept through, rustling the trees.

"—Welcome, little one, to a world frantic about the end but yet one without salvation. I welcome you."

"It doesn't sound like you're welcoming her."

"It's fiiine. It's a predecessor's obligation and right to teach children about reality."

"You're terrible."

"I sure am."

As they chatted, the two faeries both peered at the snoozing girl's face.

"I wonder what kind of dreams she's having?" said one faerie, poking the girl's chubby cheek.

"Who knows. Well, I mean, *she's* the only one who knows."

"Oh. That was a little smile just now. Is it a good dream?"

"I sure hope so."

It had been two weeks since the faerie warehouse received the message.

Some wailed, some seemed calm on the surface, some reeled, some looked on blankly, some disappeared to hunt bears—

It took two weeks for everyone to sort out their feelings.

"Aaargh!"

The sun was close to setting over the playing field at the faerie warehouse.

Tiat Siba Ignareo gave a confident cheer as she ran laps by herself around the field.

"You can push yourself, but it won't really give you a better time."

She didn't even look back when Ithea sighed at her, concentrating on nothing but running forward, pushing her steps one in front of the other.

Clinging to her chest was a silver brooch, which was still a little too big for her.

"She sure is working hard." Nygglatho approached them, and Ithea turned her head only slightly toward her.

"It also feels like she's a little too enthusiastic, though."

After the incident, Nygglatho had given herself a drastic haircut.

The little ones pestered her as to why, and all she gave was the vague answer of "Just a little change of mood," but that of course wasn't the reason. She had sent all her cut hair off with the wind from the port, scattering it to the surface. In the old troll custom, two people taking part of the other's flesh was a ceremony that tied them together forever.

"She hasn't accepted yet that Chtholly's never coming back. 'S why she's desperate to make herself as close to her as possible."

"That brings back memories. Chtholly was like that once." Nygglatho made a fragile smile. "The sadness of losing an older-sister figure became her spring, and she became incredibly strong."

"And thus the world keeps turning, huh," Ithea said carelessly, throwing herself backward onto the ground. "Nopht and the others are out of the hospital next week, right? Should we throw a welcome back party?"

"Yes. I know we're still sad about the girls who couldn't come home, but we should be happy to welcome back the ones who did."

"Man, you're so grown-up..." Ithea kicked her feet and stared at the distant sky above her. "...I guess it's about time for me to learn from you, huh?"

There was a faint glint in her eyes as she murmured to herself.

"I just dooooooon't get it."

Nopht grumbled, sitting with her feet apart on the white sheets and resting her chin on her knees.

Nopht and Rhantolk, who survived the battle on the surface, had both been thrown into another island's clinic by the airship crew members, their entire bodies injured and their life forces depleted as a result of venenum overuse. They spent several days on the brink of death. It was only very recently that they could finally sit up and talk.

"What the hell did she mean, *'I have always been happy'*? Did she think that would make me understand her? Hooray, she scattered to the wind beautifully, and we lived happily ever after? Nothing about this is happy at all, damn it!"

"Nopht, be quiet," Rhantolk said coolly, flipping through a local newspaper. "Happiness is something that only the person in question can see, something only they can understand. Only fools and selfish individuals try to decide or deny what that is for them."

"Well, *sorry* for being a fool," Nopht raged.

"…But I understand…"

…From time to time, it is the foolish and the selfish who make others happy and find happiness themselves. But Rhantolk didn't finish her sentence and just closed her eyes.

Rhantolk hadn't liked Chtholly very much. But that didn't mean she hated her all that much, either. And that's why she thought:

At the very end, if Chtholly really was as happy as she'd declared, then maybe that was the best ending she could have hoped for.

The winter sky extended for eternity.

The stars began to twinkle silently, replacing the light of the setting sun and the lost cerulean sky.

—Or maybe this was the end of just one story.

†

It was someone's dream world.

Full of phantasms, a world that couldn't possibly be real.

A nostalgic scent tickled his nose. Bread with nuts in it. Scrambled eggs. Crispy salad. Freshly squeezed oranges.

It was the smell of morning—what else could it be?

It was the scent of the beginning of the day, one so familiar to him he felt no longing for it.

"Mm…"

He stirred briefly.

"Oh, are you finally up?"

He could hear the faint sound of slippers slapping against the floor. He knew the sound of these footsteps so well.

Slowly, he opened his eyes. He could see the faded plaster on the ceiling.

"This is—"

It looked a lot like somewhere he once knew. It was very similar to a place he once wanted to go home to.

Joy welled up deep inside his heart. But something inside those depths strongly rejected the joy. This couldn't be. It shouldn't be.

"Almaria."

"Hmm?"

He called her name, and he received a response. The inside of his mind still felt murky.

"Was I asleep?"

"You seemed to be having a tough time of it. Nightmares?"

Small presences began to make themselves known throughout the building. The smell of morning struck equally each and every one who lived in the orphanage. Soon, one after the other, the children would leave their rooms and come down the stairs to show themselves.

Had he been dreaming? Could it be?

It was an incredibly realistic dream if it was. In his dream, he found himself on the brink of death countless times. He lost so much, gained so much, then lost it all again. He was so sad that the tears wouldn't come. But he was also so happy to the point that he couldn't manage a smile.

Despite how vivid dreams could be, in the end, they were nothing but dreams. He would always wake up from them. They would melt in the morning light and be forgotten. He knew that his memory of it, of something so precious to him, would soon sink into a deep place in his heart, and he would never remember it again.

You're fine with that, right? someone deep in his heart whispered to him. *Forget everything.*

"—I could never." He waved away the invitation with his still-murky reasoning.

He should wash his face to make himself feel alert. Good idea. He sat up from the couch.

A small girl rolled off his stomach.

"…Ow."

A girl with ashen-colored hair sat up as she complained disinterestedly. She rubbed her eyes and looked around.

"Huh? Where is this? Why am I…?"

Willem knew this girl. He recognized her. He remembered her. It was Nephren Ruq Insania. A leprechaun. She lived at the faerie warehouse. She was one of the protectors of Regule Aire.

"……Oh—"

Off came the lid. Once he remembered one thing, the rest came quickly. Like a forceful pull on a string, he saw images replay in his mind, one after the other. Conscious of his own deep confusion, Willem called to her:

"Nephren…?"

It was five hundred years too early to find this girl on the surface.

He called the name of the girl who should not have been there.

*   *   *

He would have noticed right away had he been a little more levelheaded.

He would have noticed the small chunk of metal emitting a soft light sitting on top of his rapidly beating heart.

That was the language comprehension talisman. It was an ancient (?) treasure, one that conveyed someone's very intentions through language. Once it was activated, one did not need to kindle any more venenum. Regardless of the user's intentions, it would convert all words directed to the user. It once helped Willem in his daily life just after he'd woken up in Regule Aire and didn't understand the official language at all, and it was now starting to work again.

No matter what anyone said, Willem Kmetsch was still a seasoned hero. His old self would have noticed right away exactly what that light meant. What exactly it meant for the world he was seeing right now. It would have shown him everything. But now—

"Mm... Hmm?"

He couldn't hear Nephren's voice as she looked around, puzzled.

"Dad? What's wrong, Dad?"

He couldn't hear Almaria's slippered feet approaching.

He couldn't see anything, couldn't think anything.

He was in a world that was neither dream nor reality, just a blank white world—

And all he could feel was the distant warmth of a tear rolling down his cheek.

Afterword /
Of Course It's an Afterword

I like stories that make us notice things.

I like stories where, upon reading it over from the beginning, I end up smacking my cheek and exclaiming, "So *that's* what that was!" Cost-effective books that can be read over and over are great, too. So I really hope the story I'm writing can be enjoyed in the same way.

Long time no see—this is Kareno.

...And as you can see, we've continued! We've made it this far! I think we've come to a really bad stopping point, but in a way, that's how it always is (how awful)!

With this and that, I now present to you Book Three of *WorldEnd*, even though I said I didn't know if I could in the afterword of the last volume!

Seriously, just between you and me, if I may be so blunt, this series was actually not supposed to keep going at one point. I was sort of vaguely thinking to myself, *Hmm, maybe I should switch gears and write an absurdly cheerful story.* I managed to get all this way only because of all the readers who decided to stick with me through the first two volumes. Again, thank you so much!

By the way, I actually didn't used to like butter cake very much.

I think it's because long ago, when I was a kid, I ate a very terrible one at a homestay once. It felt like cheap butter was slathered all over my tongue, and there was too much for me to stomach, and my host was just sitting there smiling as she watched me eat, so my eyes watered as I ate it. I finished the whole thing. I really could not stand butter cake after that.

But since I was starting to write this story, I thought, *Why not?* and bought one at a nearby store. It was so fluffy, and I ate it as I worked on the early developments in the story. It was seriously delicious. My eyes were glittering as I wrote.

Man, butter cake really is the best. I think I'll go out and get another one when I finish writing this afterword.

Next time, the past, present, and future will all meet, and his story, her story, and the girls' story will all start heading toward the same conclusion—at least, I hope we can reach that point.

Summer 2015
AKIRA KARENO

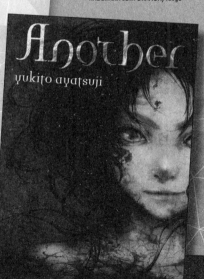